AF492450

# Mean Tales and Other Lives

Unkind Stories from this World and Others

N.W. Twyford

Copyright © 2020 N W Twyford

The right of N W Twyford to be identified as the Author of the Work has been asserted by him in accordance with the Copyright, Designs, and Patent Act 1988.

Visit nwtwyford.com or follow @nwtwyford on Twitter or Instagram for more stories and posts.

Contents

Book One: Mean Tales:



Book Two: Other Lives

# Book One:

# Mean Tales

## Sign of the Chimes

I don't think anyone really knew what changes would come when Big Ben stopped ringing. Presumably they just expected what was entirely reasonable: a very large bell in a very large clock rang no more and wouldn't for another five years. That's what the government said, that it needed to be silenced for maintenance, and so it disappeared behind a veil of scaffolding, the chimes muted.

But something else happened too. It wasn't easy to understand at first and drawing the link – the causality – between one event and those that followed it was neither easy nor obvious. But it was definitely there.

It's important you understand this.

The reaction to the bell being silenced for maintenance and restoration reasons was met with a very British mild disappointment; the people accepted it and got on with their lives. Some – myself included – wondered what this might mean for events like the two minutes silence on the 11th November. But we got on and dealt with it. It wasn't such a huge inconvenience, after all.

So, the bell was silenced, and that was that.

It wasn't long afterwards that something strange started to happen.

The first thing people noticed was that the usual bullshit they heard from politicians no longer seemed to satisfy them. It had never satisfied them, not really, but they often found themselves unable to reply, or dispute what had been said for reasons they were unsure of.

The mix of their authority, the way they presented their argument – be it endless streams of facts from allegedly renowned sources, or just repeating the same slogan over and over again until the people conceded the point – it had always seemed to be sufficient, accepted in a strange fog of inarticulate confusion that led to compliance.

When the bells stopped, so did this.

Politicians found they suddenly had to work for a living. Perhaps it's cynical to say that they weren't beforehand, but regardless of one's stance towards them, no one could argue their jobs were any easier now. Nothing they said was taken at face value any more.

The people were *awake*. They expressed their dissatisfaction with the world around them through petitions, marches and demonstrations. No amount of social media or reality TV would satisfy them.

But it wasn't just those in power the people were becoming aware of.

And that was the worst part of all.


"Lord Comely," the assistant said, stepping into his master's wood panelled room, "It's him again, on the phone."

"Thank you Stallibrass," the older man nodded. He was staring out of the large window onto the London park below. It was a nice day, all things considered. A crisp winter morning. He watched men in suits pass through the park on their way to work, off to keep the wheels turning. *As the world should be,* he thought, knowing it was a lie. "He's eager, isn't he?"

"It's the fifth time in two days," Stallibrass informed him. "I'm afraid he's getting rather terse."

"Yes," Lord Comely smiled. "I imagine he's quite used to getting his way, and between all this and an old fart like me refusing to take his calls he's probably a bit pissed."

"Yes, sir," Stallibrass nodded, wise enough not to express an opinion on his employer's behaviour one way or another. He did not mention that for years Lord Comely had moaned about being cut out of the loop, that he had grand plans for this country, if only someone would listen to him. Now someone *did* want to listen to him, and he wasn't interested.

"Let's keep him waiting a little longer, shall we, hmm?" Comely said kindly, turning to his assistant. "I suppose you're wondering what all this is about."

"It's not my place to wonder, sir," Stallibrass said, retaining his composure. He wasn't anywhere near as reserved as he let on, but he knew what Lord Comely liked from an assistant, and the close-lipped, professional routine seemed to fit the bill.

"But you *have* been wondering," Comely grinned, wryly. If Lord Comely was to be realised as an animal in animation or caricature, he would be a fox or wolf, no doubt. A fat wolf, but a wolf, nonetheless.

"I —" Stallibrass conceded, immediately regretting letting the cracks show.

"Ah! And you should be curious, yes. Although of course curiosity can be a dangerous thing, can it not? Sit." He gestured at the chair placed on the other side of the leather padded desk that lay between them. Stallibrass hesitated momentarily, then, seeing his employer was serious, took a seat. The first and last time he'd sat in this office, it had been for his interview, when Lord Comely had sized him up like a steak. Between that and the man on the phone, unprecedented events were happening all over.

In silence, Lord Comely reached into his desk. He withdrew two glasses, and two bottles. One bottle was whisky, and cost more than Stallibrass earned in a week. The other bottle was black, and unmarked. He placed a glass in front of himself and his assistant.

"Uh, sir, it's a little, I mean –" Stallibrass faltered.

"Oh, blast the time," Lord Comely scoffed, pouring them both a shot of whisky. "I never got the hang of day drinking, if I'm honest. Thought I'd try it, seemed to work for Churchill. But he lived in a very different time to this. Very different. Cheers."

He knocked the whisky back in a single hit, his face forming a grimace that perfectly displayed his large, immaculate teeth. They remained unstained, despite the booze and the cigars.

"It's to do with the bells, you see," Lord Comely began, unprompted. He poured himself another glass, rolling it around gently, as if searching for wonders that lay in the amber liquid. "I warned him, when I first heard that they planned to silence Big Ben. Me and several others. Hargraves, Willison, Pike. Yes," he beamed, seeing the look of recognition on his assistant's face as he drew the connection. "All fossils. All dead now. Of course, the fact they're gone and that they warned him aren't coincidences. No, not at all.

I'm just here because it takes more than that to finish me off," he chose to sip the whisky this time, and nodded as he swallowed, as if agreeing with it.

"He thought we were just being, I don't know. Sentimental? Precious? Something like that. We were the oldest Members of Parliament, men whose time had passed and who, in our hearts didn't really understand *why* the chimes had to be honoured; but remembered when *we* were young, the old claimed silencing them would bring ruin." He smiled again. "I say 'in our hearts,' but I don't think Hargraves had one. Bitter old bastard, may he rot in hell.

"They laughed at us, of course. Him, on the phone out there, and all his cronies. The new blood. It's to be expected really. We laughed at the old farts when they mentioned it to us, all those decades ago, but I suppose it must have stuck, or we wouldn't have said anything. But at least we did it behind their backs. It showed some respect. I can't begin to tell you how angry it made me, to be dismissed so easily. Mocked. Treated like a superstitious old hag, preaching disaster. Well, look who's on the phone now!"

Stallibrass fidgeted, as if reminded exactly *who* was on the phone, and the fact he was being kept waiting really was most unheard of.

"Oh, let's keep him hanging on a bit longer," Comely smiled. He looked down his nose at his assistant's glass. "You've not touched your drink."

"Oh. No," Stallibrass said, apologetically, taking a sip. The gold liquid was exceptionally potent, made far worse for drinking it at this hour. The frost had yet to vanish in the sun, and here they were, sipping whisky. He supressed a shudder as it slipped down his throat.

"That was their mistake," Comely continued. "They had forgotten how important the damned bells were. They're only just starting to see now." He took a deep, loving sip of the whisky and grinned. "Ah! That's good stuff. I've been saving this, you know. I daren't tell you for how long. Anyway, soon enough, they'll be praying for the five years to pass, for Big Ben to chime once more. Those who are left, that is. Oh yes, not everyone will make it to the end. Not by a long shot."

There was a pause, as Lord Comely stared off. It stretched on, until only the clicking of the grandfather clock could be heard. When Stallibrass was finally about to speak, his master said abruptly, "Of course, what they'll all pray *to* is best not discussed. And that's part of the problem."

He turned to his assistant; eyes wide. "The others didn't know, but I do. I made it my business to learn. Someone had to know. The bells have tolled for over one hundred and fifty years. In that time the world had become more rational, more civilised, and less superstitious. It had become safer and smarter, or that's what we wanted it to believe. The truth is, that's not it at all. It has been lied to, and the bells mask the lies.

"You wait," Comely said, pointing a chubby finger at the younger man. "Keep an eye on the news, no matter how dubious the source. Watch the tone shift. The strange and the sinister will start to become noticed. Mysteries that no one has ever really paid attention to, or at least questioned before, will present themselves, and no easy answers will be able to explain them."

He set the drink down.

"Nor will they stop."

"Sir," Stallibrass began, "I'm afraid I don't –"

"Some of the occurrences will be new: things not seen before and devised by minds only recently driven to such ends. If I had to guess, they'll be acts of desperation, in some cases of hastily covering tracks, whereas others will be those who are unable to stop. They'll be messy."

The older man picked up his drink again, as if he couldn't be without it for long. There was an agitation to his movements, as if he was somewhat excited. He considered the liquor for a moment, before knocking it back and smacking his lips with a satisfying, "Ah!" Thoughtfully, he set the glass down, and his tone darkened. His eyes bored into his assistant, as if what he was about to say mattered more than anything that preceded it.

"The majority will be the work of ancient things with old hates," he said, matter-of-factly, "That long-ago forged pacts with those in power for their mutual benefit. From what I gather, the agreement was simple. Binding. The powerful stayed that way, and the things that could not be named were promised anonymity, discretion, and compliance. That was what the bells were for, you see. To stop people noticing. Don't ask me how, but they were. And in silencing them, the pact has been violated. So now, as ever, these angry, hateful things move unchecked in the world, and death follows in their wake. The difference is, now they're going to start being noticed."

The old man stopped there. He let his gaze linger on his assistant, who sat in silence. Stallibrass hadn't truly understood what his employer had been saying, but each and every word had left its mark on his memory. It didn't matter whether he thought the old man to be drunk, insane, or quite possibly telling the truth. The weight behind his words would be enough to make him remember this.

"And that's all I'll tell you," Lord Comely said patiently, as if he'd finished telling a bedtime story. "I think that should do. I'll speak to him now."

"Him?" Stallibrass sputtered, remembering who had been waiting on the phone all this time. "Sir, he'll be gone for sure!"

"Oh no," Comely said, waving a hand dismissively, "He'll want to speak to me, mark my words. Not that he'll want to hear what I have to say, of course. Best put him through."

Stallibrass rose. His legs felt like lead. He glanced down at his drink. Some remained in the glass. He weighed up his choices, and then on impulse, reached down and knocked it back. It seemed like the thing to do.

"Good man!" Lord Comely said approvingly, clapping his great hands together.

Stallibrass nodded and started to walk out the room.

"Oh, Stallibrass…?" his employer called after him. He turned.

"When they ask you about what we discussed, you're best off telling them I was sloshed, that I rambled, and you don't remember anything specific. You'll be safer that way."

"When who ask, sir?" Stallibrass frowned.

"Thank you Stallibrass, that'll be all."

Still not understanding, the assistant left the room.

While he waited, Lord Comely returned the bottle of whisky to the draw. The black bottle remained, and he removed the stopper. There was no point drinking this from a glass, he'd have to neck as much of it as he could while he was able. First though, it was time to have a little chat.

Finally, the phone buzzed. He picked up the receiver.

"Hello," he smiled, "So sorry to keep you waiting."

There was a pause as the voice on the line spoke its piece.

"No, it's as we discussed, I'm afraid," he said, gravely. Another pause. "No, I couldn't say how long. That'll depend on whether the siren at Broadmoor hospital is still active. If not, the epicentre will be around there. I warned you about that too, if you'll recall."

Hearing what the other voice had to say, Lord Comely brought the black bottle to his lips. "Ah," he sighed.

"Well, then I'm afraid you're fucked, Prime Minister."

*The whistles sound a bit like screams*, Tom thought, sometimes. They were certainly shrill enough.

He had heard them, on certain nights, his entire life. The trains.

Always late at night, when his family slept. Sometimes when it was clear, when the moon washed his bedroom in silver light, and at other times when it rained; the sounds magnified maybe, carried through the downpour. He didn't know why. He didn't stop to think about it.

Their sound – the chugging and the whistles left no doubt – these were steam trains.

But no steam trains ran anymore on the only line that passed nearby, he had checked. He had researched the line and its history thoroughly, becoming something of an obsession to him. The services were cancelled years ago, a thing of years gone by.

So what was it Tom heard, on these seemingly random nights when he smoked out his window without his parents knowing? The mystery gnawed at him, and he knew he had to learn more.

Tom waited until his parents were asleep before going out, telling them he was going to stay up and watch the late night film, keeping an ear open for the sounds of slumber.

He left the house, walked through the gentle suburbs and entered the woods past the train station, the entrance winding round the back of a small industrial estate.

Tom made his way deep into Ambarrow woods. He knew them well, having gone in there innumerable times throughout his life. First on night hikes with the Cubs, then as he got older, climbing the hill with his friends. They used to play on the rope swing, and, as interests changed, it became a great location to build a fire and get high. The guitars would eventually come out, and Tom would feel obliged to give his forcibly growly rendition of *Wish You Were Here*.

The woods were empty tonight, and he fought off a sense of paranoia, flinching at every sound.

There was one point in the woods where the path crossed the railway tracks, the route gently leading down to the railway with a surprising lack of fuss. There was no bridge, markings or precautions; just an understanding that one would cross without incident or dawdling.

Tom respected that. It gave him a sense of nostalgia for a time he had never lived in, that he had only seen in films and read about in books.

Alone, he waited by the tracks for the mystery train.

*

Time passed, and Tom settled into an uneasy routine of boredom and, well, feeling a bit weird. It wasn't the sort of thing one told their friends about. In his mind, he figured it was somewhere between stargazing and dogging. It was definitely closer to the former, but that aspect of lurking, even if not sexual, made him feel like he was doing something strange.

Eventually, Tom realised he had wasted his time. All he had achieved was a walk, and cramp in his knees from squatting.

*Fuck this.*

He got up, dusting himself off and slowly making his way back up the hill, away from the tracks.

That was when he heard it.

The whistle was shrill and pure, cutting through the still night air. It was just like he had always heard, but so much louder and clearer.

Tom ran back to the tracks, and waited.

He saw the smoke first. The moonlight caught it, making it resemble a thick mass of low hanging cloud; pumped skywards with the machine precision that was expected of it.

*I knew it*, Tom thought, as he waited for the mysterious train to get closer. Steam trains were for exhibitions, for events. For *showing off*. Why would any make their way along the track at this time of night? He watched, wondering, as the train chugged closer, its sound and movement embracing every cliché of its type.

Illuminated by the moonlight, the train was easier to see now. As it came into view, Tom thought he saw something strange. Everything else was as he expected, but this one detail…

*It looked like –*

*No –*

*Wait, I think it is –*

*Oh bloody hell –*

The train had a *face*.

Seemingly grey – although in this light, who could say for sure – it wasn't painted on, but appeared to be affixed to the front of the train somehow. It was grossly distorted, its proportions stretched, as if it had once been the size of a man's face, but had been pulled to become something else entirely.

It grew closer, and the more Tom stared, the more he noticed. It wasn't flat; the face had all the contours of one wrapped around a skull, manipulated by muscle. It seemed to smile, he saw, and the toy-like eyes were large and stupid, happily content in its own strange world.

Tom had already stepped back from the tracks as the train went past. For some reason, he didn't want it to see him, as absurd as that sounded. The train whistled just before it went by, and Tom could have sworn he glimpsed the face contort, as if in pain.

*Whistles that sound like screams.*

Tom looked for a driver, but couldn't see one. He saw the open cabin, and the orange light of the stove burning coal, but no man could be seen within.

The train towed wooden bodied carriages with steamed up windows. Tom could see people inside, silhouettes moving strangely in the gloom. Each carriage contained a different type of passenger, and as the lights flickered on and off, he caught glimpses of them.

Within the first carriage people were eating. Eating was putting it kindly; these people were stuffing their faces, taking entire fistfuls of food and shoving it into their mouths without discretion or dignity.

Inside the second carriage was fighting; passengers attacking one another without remorse, savagely. Bodies bounced off cracked glass, chairs were thrown, and – Tom was sure – he saw passengers wielding cutlery as weapons. The inside of one of the windows was splattered with something dark.

The people in the third carriage seemed to be engaged in an orgy. He first noticed this when he saw hands pressed against the glass, flat palms wiping the condensation as they were forced against them. Tom craned his neck to look within this one and quickly regretted it: the orgy was violent, the figures within moving with an obsessive lust that showed aggression and hatred, devoid of passion. It made him feel sick.

The remaining carriages passed, and Tom watched them all with interest and an increasing sense of disgust. One was filled with people stripping the carriage bare, scrabbling and fighting over everything they could lay their hands on. In another, passengers barely moved at all, stretched out apathetically, as if heavily sedated. The carriages went on, each one distinctive from the last.

Tom watched them all go, deep unease shivering across his skin.

The train moved down the line, slowing, and after hesitating, Tom followed, running down the track in its wake. After a short while, the track split, and the train went down a diverted line, into darkness.

Tom had taken this line scores of times, and never once had he known of a diverted route: as far as he knew, the train went from Reading to Shalford, and that was it. He didn't even know of any other routes that intersected with it.

The tracks shouldn't be there.

Which was why he kept repeating, *You're a fucking idiot,* over and over, in his head. Why that pit of anxiety that grew in his belly went deeper and deeper, mirroring the darkness he was descending into as he followed the train, the only light coming from the ghastly carriages that cast shoddy, shadow strewn images onto the ground around it.

He kept going like that for some time, trying to stay on the sleepers to avoid tripping, when lights came from ahead, and the route opened out. Tom had no choice but to follow close behind; with the edges of the line opening he was exposed, the carriage his only cover.

He was in a railway yard.

The tracks were a spider's web of lines, lit by sickly white light from ancient lampposts.

The yard was *alive*. All over, black shapes with yellow eyes – things that were meant to be men but couldn't be, not from their shapes or the way they moved – were at work, but when the train came to a halt, pulling up at a desolate platform, they stopped what they were doing and descended on the carriages in a black mass.

They hauled the passengers out. Those who had been consumed by their desires came out of their trances; some filthy, others bloodied, some naked. Some were all three, and as they realised where they were, what state they were in and what was happening, terror struck them.

A deep, booming voice yelled, ordering the shapes: "All change please!"

Tom had seen more than enough. He wanted to run, but fear froze him into place. If he stayed hidden – even with the shapes only feet away from him – he could remain unseen. But he knew he couldn't remain there much longer.

*Fuck it, just go –*

He ran, feet moving so fast he almost tripped. Tightness seized his chest and adrenaline failed to carry him anywhere near as far as he hoped –

*Keep going, don't stop –*

The darkness of the way he came loomed, for once inviting, better the devil he knew.

He was close, almost out, when more black shapes emerged from the darkness, cutting him off. "No trespassing!" he heard behind him, the same voice that boomed orders to the shapes.

The man was well dressed in a top hat and tails, massively obese, but strength radiated from his enormous frame. His face was beyond hideous.

The black shapes surrounded Tom, clutching at him, with a cold and firm grip. He wrestled, but more hands came to grasp him.

"Get off me!" Tom snapped, struggling. He might as well have tried fighting the tide.

"Please –"

"You haven't paid your fare!" the controller of the shapes screamed.

"I didn't ride the train! I followed it!"

"You have caused confusion and delay!" the Controller said, "But you will be useful!"

*

Tom woke to wind blowing in his face, which felt strange, tingling, and slightly numb.

It was still night. Everything was a blur around him, and as his eyes focused, he realised it wasn't his eyes, it was everything else.

It was moving. *He* was moving.

The wind hurt his eyes, yet no tears came. He tried to move his face out of the wind, but he couldn't. It was fixed in place, somehow.

So was the rest of him. He tried to move his hands, but they didn't seem to work.

All he could see was the tracks, passing beneath him.

Tom screamed, but nothing came from his throat. Instead, a shrill whistle cried behind him. He couldn't see what it was, but he suspected.

Panic started to overtake Tom. He wanted to get off whatever he was on, but of course he could not.

But underneath the chill of terror was a warmth. Something calm and nurturing stoked in his belly, bringing peace despite the horror he felt.

Tom knew what he could feel burning, what calmed him. It was his soul. The engine was consuming his soul, burning it like coal.

It didn't make sense, but then, nothing did. How else could Tom explain what was happening, what he was becoming?

Except…

… He wanted to be called Thomas now. It had a better ring to it.

And the engine behind him, that *was* him, continued to eat into his soul, chewing it around.

But he didn't mind. He didn't mind anything.

All he could think was how he wanted to be a really useful engine.

*Chew chew.*

## The Vacant Field

There's that field off the motorway. You know the one, don't you? You do, even though there's no reason why you should. It just came into your head. It does that, although it doesn't want to be noticed. You can see it from the road, not far from the junction. It's an odd shape, but surely it could be used for something, couldn't it?

Or maybe… maybe you can tell that there's something... *off* about it. You'd be right. Take it from me. It was in my family for generations, for further back than anyone can remember. It came into our possession when things were different, when they were good. But things change. I'm the last of this line, now, and when I'm gone it will be like we never were. Even though the field is no longer ours, I feel we're still linked, and I wonder if when I'm dead, whether the field will be too.

I doubt it. But I hope.

You don't understand. Let me explain.

The field in question was once part of a larger plot of land owned by a wealthy landowner, my ancestor. It gave good yield and was profitable. No different than any other.

Then the killings happened. The victims were young. Beautiful. These were sex crimes, heinous and unforgivable, the sort of things considered horrific to even imagine, let alone speak aloud. I tried learning what they were, back when I thought I could change things. I learned only a little, and what I did discover sickened me to my core, to a place where I chose to no longer try and fathom them. The choice was between understanding (and madness), or ignorance. It was too late for the latter. I chose repression, and for the most part I am successful. My understanding of what happened that night – so many years before I was born – comes to me sometimes, when I'm struggling to sleep, or when my defences are lowered, staring deep into the fire in the dark, trying to understand how things came to be this way. And as I piece it back to that night, and the fate of the innocents, when the light of recognition illuminates even the slightest corner of the image, I turn away, trying my best not to have seen too much.

Sometimes I'm sick afterwards. Sometimes from the horror, other times because in my desperation, I seek to purge the knowledge from my body, and want it gone by any means necessary.

I won't tell you what happened, so don't ask. You know all you need to. The important thing is that it happened. To them. The sin of it seeped into the marrow of the land, into the roots. The water table.

Deep under the earth, it festered into hate.

Soon enough, the field stopped being productive, and every time the landowner tried to grow anything from it, only disaster took root. Many accidents befell the farmhands who tried to tilde the land, even from those who were experienced or expert. It seemed to be more trouble than it was worth, and when the harvest came – and all the crops turned out to be blighted – the landowner turned it over to livestock. The results were far worse.

Horses broke their legs in droves, the field seeming to welcome the sound of their screams as their legs snapped. The holes that tripped them could never be found. Scores of the beasts had to be put down, their elegance and grace lost in their cries and flails.

He tried again with less precious stock. Sheep met as unpleasant an end; *something* coming in the night and eviscerating them. This was not the work of foxes or wolves, the creatures did not appear to be fed upon, simply dismembered, or perhaps worse, hurt for the sake of it.

Gorse and brambles took root, anything that was coarse or unwelcoming; the bodies of small animals becoming caught in the tangle of thorns. Some drowned when the field flooded; others were eaten alive; many simply starved to death, becoming part of the rot.

Not even crows landed in the field, for not even carrion was safe in it.

It didn't take the landowner long to realise: *this field was cursed.* These were superstitious times. The only thing that would be harvested from the field was tragedy. He learned this to his cost.

He knew he should never, ever try and yield anything from the field again.

It was sectioned off, the blighted corner isolated, the convenience of a simpler shape be damned, as the field itself was.

Years passed. Men grew old and died. The landowner retired, passing his property onto his sons. The eldest was just old enough to remember the grief the field brought, how his father associated tending it with the tragedies that beset his life. He was not superstitious, but he was wise, and he knew his father was no fool. If they could afford to leave the field untouched, they would.

And so life went on, until times grew tough and the son, who had grown old and infirm, left the lands to his son-in-law to tend. The son-in-law – my grandfather – was practically minded and had not heard the tales of the field. He tried to grow crops. They suffered blight. Some carried poison. Livestock went blind, mad, miscarried, or died. Accidents happened on the field ugly and unfathomable. Grim things, involving heavy and sharp tools.

Then one day: tragedy. My grandfather brought his family in to clear the field once and for all. These men knew what they were doing, and would not be stopped by a square of mud.

They should have left well alone. Trying to free his tools from an entanglement of brambles, his eldest son caught his feet in the same mess of thorns, his movements serving somehow to constrict them around his ankles. In other circumstances, he might have been able to free himself, but under the brambles, a bog had spread, and opened up to let him sink in. The stinking marsh pulled him under, and the brambles stopped him fighting free.

My grandfather tried in vain to save him, but could only watch as his son was consumed, claimed by the vacant field; stinking, filthy water pouring into his open mouth and smothering his screams as he sank.

And so, I never met my uncle.

It was at this point that my grandfather sought out his father-in-law. He could hardly bear to tell the old man his grandson's fate, for the sight was too painful for him to recall, and he worried the sheer horror of it would threaten to send him into the next world.

His father-in-law steeled himself as he listened, and then with quivering hands and tears in his eyes, recounted the history of the vacant field, and the terrible thing that had happened there all those years ago, terrified to learn, at the very end of his life, that evil was real, and had lashed out at his family.

My grandfather's father-in-law, my great grandfather, died in the night, his heart having stopped abruptly.

As if my grandfather needed any further encouragement, he decided then and there no one would ever use the field and suffer the fate that had befallen him. Wills were drawn up which guaranteed it would not be used.

More time went by. The fortunes of the family changed, shifted, were squandered. I was not born into the wealth of those who came before me, and in my youth, much of our land was sold, including the fields connected to the cursed one.

In dividing the Estate, the lawyers saw what had been written in times past, and understood that it was still binding, even if it confused them. For completion's sake they decided it was time to let the field go. It earned and brought nothing. To keep it was an inconvenience. It was only paperwork, after all.

And so, the field left my family's possession for the first time in centuries, sold to a trust.

It was around this time that I came of age, and desired to learn of my family's history. My grandfather had died, and through his letters, I came to piece together my family's past connection with this one, strange, unfortunate plot of land. It was one quirk in an otherwise unremarkable history, and it piqued my interest.

I learned what I could, and I kept an eye on the field.

At first, all seemed well. Perhaps the troubles were behind us. The trust knew the terms of the sale, and it suited their ethos.

But the contract had limits. It was not future proofed. It did not anticipate green energy, nor creative farming methods.

The honey was acrid, toxic. The sloes made poisonous gin. But worst of all, the energy that was sold, if it could be traced back, led to ruin. It failed to fulfil hospital equipment, brain damaging coma patients, staggering release rates in drips, muting alarms when heart rates dropped on monitors.

People died. Old and young. Some very young.

Some of those that did not die but lived should not have lived. For living was a punishment for them.

The connection was made and the power obtained from the field was pulled.

And that was that.

For now.

The age of superstition is over, no one would care for old tales. No one had a gut instinct, no trail to follow. No sacrifices would be made in the field, no attempts to appease old sins would be tried. Nothing was dug up, burned, exhumed. No wrongs were put right.

And yet.

I know none of these things would make a difference, this isn't that sort of evil. But I visited that hospital. I saw parents holding brain damaged babies, I saw people who would never wake up, and I saw broken things that would never be fixed. I saw what the vacant field could do.

I'm going out in that field tonight. Because we're linked, as much as a person and a piece of earth can be. Our destinies are entwined through blood and history.

I need to see for myself the damage that old hate has wrought, and to understand how something can be made of such malice, and dispel or purge it, if I can.

I say that like it's going to happen, but it won't. I'm old now, old enough to know the way the world works but not so old I can just let it be.

And I know, most likely, that I will die in this field. They might find my body the next day, perhaps a week later, perhaps never. I leave this note behind me for those who may wonder what happened to me, and more importantly, as a warning to those who may wish to exploit the field in future.

And then, when I'm gone, a field, a vacant plot of land will remain untouched. It will return to the wild, to wallow in its hate and rot.

And will continue to do so until the end of time.

## The Four

*They're Horsemen*, the Survivor thought, with all the certainty of a man who had witnessed a true, logic shattering atrocity.

*They're Horsemen and they're all our fault.*

He had staggered out of the burning remnants of the compound and towards the shore, where waves lapped at the coast, ignorant to the horror that had occurred only several hundred metres away. He did not know if any of the others had made it out alive. All he knew was that things had gone very, very wrong.

They *had* to be Horsemen, he thought, suspecting that his sanity was cracked, perhaps broken. Only Horsemen could bring the end of the world in such a way.

The yellow one was Famine, the colour of wilted crops. The green was Pestilence, the shade of infection. The red was War for the blood that flows. And the last, a purple so dark it was almost black. That one was Death.

*They didn't exactly…* look *like Horsemen though,* he thought briefly, before the observation passed with a bitter choke of a laugh. It didn't matter. They brought ruin: that was all that mattered.

The Survivor still carried the hypodermic loaded with the sedative, just in case he had to use it. The gesture was, of course, futile. There would be no way he could use it.

Not on them, but it had other purposes.

Loading up his pockets with as many stones as they would bear, he waded in as far up to his waist. The water was shockingly cold.

He removed the cap on the syringe and pressed the needle's tip to his wrist. He did not struggle to find the vein; his pulse was racing, the veins surging with blood craving oxygen.

Depressing the stopper, he continued walking forwards before the drug took hold.

His last thought, as the waters rose around him and the feeling of utter and absolute numbness took hold was surprisingly abstract.

*What others would think of them?*

*

*They were monsters*, the Scientist thought. That's what she was there to study, and to assess, in a remote location that didn't technically exist. Proper, dyed in the wool aberrations. Part machine, so they said – although you wouldn't know it to look at them – part… something else. Flesh, of a type, but what flesh; who could say? They were ungodly. Unnatural.

She'd come to the project late, had been assigned to it because no one else could be.

There was no one left. The original team had all gone mad.

Mad might be oversimplifying it somewhat, she thought, ever rational. Certainly they were beyond use. Some were struck off, retired to quiet places in the country to live lives without consequence or stress. They would certainly contribute nothing further to science. Perhaps that was for the best, given what they had created.

One member of the team had been institutionalised, possibly never to return. His language was similar to that of the subjects; uh oh, uh oh, uh oh, over and over again, accompanied with lurches or head butts against padded walls, the movements following the same rhythm of the idiot speak. Sometimes he wouldn't stop until forcibly restrained, hair matted with his blood.

Another had opened her wrists.

And another, believing his colleagues dead, had taken a walk into the sea and never came out again.

The creatures did not know this, did not know anything, as far as the Scientist could tell. They were idiots; actual simpletons, tumbling around on their faux landscape; unawares that they were being watched, that they basked under a painted sky, a faux ceiling of Truman Show-like ingenuity. The sun was fake, and laughed at them, and they did not question that. The plants were phony, and issued orders, and they did not question that either. As far as they knew, the whole world existed for them.

It made no sense. The whole thing was naive and coddling and utterly mad.

The Scientist did not know how they had come to be; the previous team had destroyed most of their notes in a delirious haste, the fire ravaging their office, burning at least one of their number severely. Were they once apes? Some sort of bear? Surely (and this was where reason reached its end) not once man? She supposed it was best to act like it didn't matter, in terms of her studies, although that logic only sat right when accompanied by two fingers of whisky, applied on repeat.

She never used to be much of a drinker. It came easier now.

The question she'd been asked, the wrong question, but the one they were paying her for was at least one she could explore without her ethics crippling her.

What can we use them for?

*

*They were fucking useless*, thought the General. Who ever thought they would be a good idea was clearly out of their minds, he concluded, and he knew he was right, given what had happened to the first team. The new project leader, a woman who seemed permanently tired and who tried to give an objective, almost disinterested air seemed to smell more of drink and smoke the longer she was on the project for. She didn't have any answers. It was stupid to assume she would.

Their purpose eluded her, and who could blame her for failing? They were completely untrainable, even simple conditioning escaped their idiot brains; their grins fixed like skeletons. The most one could manage was getting them to go to bed, which was achieved by monotonously repeating the same, simple command, over and over again. They resisted everything else.

If they couldn't be used and they couldn't tell the public (which they couldn't, not without the most damning of inquiries) then perhaps termination was best.

Or it would be, but the damn things were indestructible. They were bullet proof, flame retardant, (flame retarded, the General joked to no one) you name it. They did not require sustenance, so God knows how they were alive. Maybe they weren't, and that was the point.

All he knew was they could trample a man to death while laughing, tear his arms off like a child pulling legs off a spider – sometimes cooing for good measure – and hug him to the point where his skull split, all the while doing a little dance. The smile never dropped once.

In all the horrors of man, war, and science, he'd never seen anything like them before.

*

*They were certainly original*, thought the Politician. He'd never seen anything like them before either.

He still wasn't entirely sure how this had come his way; a contact of a friend of a former colleague looking for a favour led its way to him, and he had a reputation for solving the sort of problems that had no right to be fixed.

He knew spin. There was no story he couldn't turn good – he prided himself on that – the trick was knowing when to start and end it, where to point the cameras, how selective you were with the facts. Every story is a snippet of reality. The trick is showing what reality you want.

An idea came to him; one so blackly funny he wanted to laugh but he didn't want to risk a thing. A way to make these abominations profitable, a way to put them to work, even if they didn't know it. They would not be engines of war, but entertainment. And entertainment was *far* more profitable than war.

You'd need to omit any human interaction whatsoever, he thought. The fear was palpable from the security tapes, even at a distance. Isolation and a cheery soundtrack should remedy it.

No kids. They'd crush them in a second, in a wave of enthusiasm. There were rumours, from the contact that something like this had happened before, had led to the team that developed them all leaving under shady and hasty circumstances. It didn't bear thinking about; the pulped remains of the infants, dragged and spread like bloody rags, used to add the missing red to a landscape of greens, blues and yellows.

He would have to make sure there was literally nothing they could destroy, because with the exception of each other, who they never seemed to get aggressive with, could they destroy a lot. Their enclosure was reinforced titanium behind the fake scenery and bright colours, tested and replaced monthly. Perhaps they didn't really want to get out; they only wanted to amble wherever their imaginations took them, and their imaginations were as limited as their intelligence.

He started to make arrangements.

*

*I don't know what the fuck they are,* the Producer thought, *but they've got potential.*

She liked the format – the four of them, each with a different colour, different shaped accessories. They were distinctive, marketable.

The Studio Head had gotten the footage from… somewhere. He wouldn't say, and the Producer was smart enough to know not to ask.

The conditions were simple and mysterious. The studio would receive the rushes, unmarked, with no correspondence or paperwork, and they could do whatever they liked with it; in fact, they were encouraged to edit it, add sound, effects, narration, you name it. Anything to make it seem less real. Anything to stop people suspecting.

As far as anyone outside the studio knew, this was their latest hit programme. All the supplier asked for was their fifty percent share of profits. They were a silent partner in this particular co-production. When you took design, costumes, actors, props, camera crews, sound and everything else out of the equation, it was quite a bargain.

*

*They were magical*, thought Timmy, two and a half, and who took a few attempts to say the word. Magical.

The characters danced, played, sang, hugged, all under a smiling sun, with blue skies and fluffy clouds and even fluffier bunnies. He sang their songs and recited their broken English. He loved them.

*

They were *weird*, thought Timmy's Mum, who didn't like them. They were repetitive and monotonous and their songs were gibberish, but hey, Timmy liked them and they kept him quiet which let her have some time to herself.

The one thought that stuck in her mind as she left Timmy in the living room, that passed by, a flicker in her consciousness, was one most parents ask from time to time.

Where do they come up with these ideas?

Control Eye

On the 1st of April a new service was quietly revealed to the world. Despite the date, it was not a joke, but you would be forgiven for thinking it was.

It called itself Control I (as in eye, not one), and that seemed to be the name of both the product and the company.

*Don't you wish you had more time?* It declared to the world.

The service Control I claimed to offer was unique. Using temporal tracking and manipulation technology, it was able to calculate the duration of a client's life and establish their date of death. This date was not given to the client in order to minimise any anxiety they might feel over knowing when they would die, or, worse, try and take steps to change their fate, potentially ensuring it became a paradox.

This was not the service they offered, by the way, it was part of the process for what followed.

What Control I did was far more enticing than that.

"Think of it like Microsoft Excel," the doctor, who insisted clients call her Donna, told Evelyn. "You use Excel, don't you?"

"Sure," said Evelyn, 32, a trader for a major investment group in the city. I won't tell you which one, but if you saw their annual profit margin, you'd realise you've been working for the wrong company for quite a while. Possibly the only problem with Evelyn's life was that she needed more time to enjoy herself, and she had the money to pay for it.

"Well, Microsoft Excel has that insert function, where you can insert as many additional lines into a document as you want. We offer a similar service, except instead of a spreadsheet, we can do that with your life."

"How does that work though?" Evelyn frowned. "How is it possible for me to get extra days if I've lived them once?"

"It's a very good question," Donna said, smiling through perfect teeth. "Without boring you with technical terminology, you identify where you would like to insert more time and how much time you would like to add. We then take this time away from the end of your life, and let you live it then, when you actually need it. The example I often give people is to imagine they're getting married next month and are a bit stressed. You want a week off beforehand, but of course there's no way you've got the time for that. We encase those seven days in a temporal seal while you live those seven days as normal, getting all that wedding prep done, and noting each and every place you go to, every interaction. We help you with this by providing you with a device that monitors what you do over that time. Otherwise," Donna chuckled, "You'd be writing down what you do all day rather than living it, and then what's the point of having that extra time? At the end of those seven days, you're sent back to the start of that period, and you live the week over. You cannot interact with anyone you already have over this period, and you have to make sure you wouldn't meet yourself in that time, but provided you do not do that, you're free to unwind before the big day."

"Okay," Evelyn nodded, picturing what she would do in that position. "I'm not exactly the marrying type."

"Neither am I, and for people like us, it's even better," Donna beamed. "Think about it: the scope is as wide as you want it to be. Take a holiday without using up your annual leave entitlement. Study something. Try an advanced cooking class. Write that novel that's inside you. Have an affair, if you really want to. Or just spend a week in your gym clothes watching television. It's entirely your call. At the end of the week, you resume your life. As far as everyone around you knows, come Monday you arrive looking like you've had the world's most relaxing weekend."

"It's tempting," Evelyn agreed, shaking her head.

"You don't have to decide now," Donna assured her. "Drawing down from your future – recouping, if you will – is a daunting process. The thought of having slightly less time than you should, even in your nineties, can be off putting for some people. Take your time and let us know."

"I'm just thinking about what my alternative would be," Evelyn said, decisively, "Enjoying myself now, or hanging around in a nursing home while I shit myself and watch daytime TV fifty years from now. I'll enjoy life while I can, cheers."

"Very good," Donna beamed. "I'll draw up the paperwork. Do you have an approximate duration of your first experience?"

It wasn't hard for Control I to arrange a week for Evelyn. There was one other caveat.

"You can't post anything you do in the inserted week on social media," Donna said. "It'll raise too many questions."

Evelyn rolled her eyes at that. She held social media in distain.

"It sounds obvious, but it's led to some messy experiences for some other clients," Donna smiled.

The first few days of the week Evelyn was going to duplicate felt very strange, as she became overly aware, almost self-conscious of who she spoke to and when.

Work colleagues were easy to compartmentalise. Out of habit she saw her girlfriend, who she wasn't especially keen on and didn't live with. She spoke to her parents. And so on. It was amazing, really, how most of these interactions were only out of a sense of obligation, she realised. None of them she'd miss being apart from for a week, that was for sure.

It was strange, she thought. Evelyn knew enough about time travel from films to know that at that moment, there was another her, a week older, who had lived this life through once and was now repeating it on her terms. She was almost tempted to try and meet her, although she knew she could not.

All the time Evelyn carried on her person a small, oval-shaped silver device that Donna referred to as a monitor, which discreetly recorded where she went and when.

She didn't feel she needed it. Evelyn deliberately ensured she had the least eventful week possible, going straight from home to work and back again. She went to the obligatory Friday night drinks with the team, but mostly because that was what was expected of her, and she didn't want to arouse suspicion. She tried to act as normal as she could throughout the drinks, but it was hard, having this secret. Donna had advised discretion.

Evelyn did not know if Control I was legal or not and didn't mind either way, she liked keeping it secret. It was part of the thrill.

*

It wasn't long before Evelyn came back to Control I.

The week alone, doing exactly what she wanted had been the perfect tonic for her life. It was amazing how much one could get done when they had literally no life admin, and no obligations.

She managed a mini break to the country, had sorted out her flat, managed to go running, and had enjoyed the obligatory sofa days watching the guilty pleasure reality TV she used to enjoy but no longer had time for. The only adjustment was leaving the flat before her past self got home from work, but given that meant nights spent in a hotel, she wasn't complaining.

"Two weeks," she stated, when she returned to the Control I offices.

And then, when she returned from that: "I want a month."

*

After she left, Donna knew exactly how this was going to go, as if she didn't already.

People were so predictable, she reflected, feeling proud. You just had to know how best to lure them in.

Control I was quite the achievement, she thought, just not in the way most people would consider. The achievement wasn't in the technology, or the profits, but the showmanship, the deception, and what it achieved.

"Is that right?" asked Mal, when they met for drinks later.

"Of course it is," Donna grinned. "There *is* no technology that can warp time like that."

"Oh," Mal said, taking a hesitant sip of his whisky. "I don't really follow human achievements since they discovered electricity. How's it done then? Dark rites? Blood magic?"

"Bit of both," she nodded. "I got the idea based on how we see time. You know that humans can only perceive time in a linear fashion, don't you?"

"Course I do," Mal sniffed. "If they could see it like we do, our job would be a lot harder."

"Exactly. But it got me thinking: they can't see time like we can, but they've got one thing we never had: free will. What if we combined the two, to a certain extent?"

"But it's not really combining it, is it?" Mal said. "If they could see their whole lives, they'd never go near our kind. You're keeping them blinkered but allowing them to make mistakes on a grander scale."

"Can't argue with that," Donna agreed. She placed a hand on her hip and wiggled her shoulders playfully. "Although taking this shape certainly helps persuade them."

"I've got to admit, Donna the curvaceous doctor is definitely less terrible to behold than Abaddon, the angel of the abyss. Or the angel of death, or the destroyer. You've a few titles, I can't keep them straight."

"Ah, fuck titles," Donna spat. "None of them matter after we were kicked out."

"True," Mal nodded. "To fucking titles and fucking humankind in inventive new ways."

Donna gave a throaty laugh and they clinked glasses.

Time was a cyclical thing to angels, fallen or otherwise. If you asked Donna or Mal, they probably wouldn't be able to tell you whether they saw every moment as one, or whether they had just lived for so long that they saw the pattern in everything. Humans were, of course, creatures of habit, and when you've been observing the same creatures over millennia, they do tend to be quite predictable. The novelty now was that technology was reaching the point where meddling with the laws of physics like this were almost fathomable to them.

So much for the age of enlightenment.

*

Off Evelyn would go, having a whale of a time, Donna explained to Mal. She had already ticked off most items from her to-do list, the normal things. She had done up her home, spent more time outdoors, caught up on her interests.

After that she would start getting a little more creative, and investigate interests as if time and money were no issue, which they weren't. Travel would probably play a significant part, because there's only so much one can experience in England.

But after that? That's where it got interesting.

Provided Donna knew her well enough – and she did, she chose her subjects for a reason – Evelyn would start looking at the darker side of life. She had an insatiable lust which no one partner, male of female, could satisfy, and with the social barriers removed and anonymity enforced, she would start to explore that in places that cater to such tastes. That's fair enough, Donna shrugged. Bit of lust never hurt anyone.

But she knew Evelyn's urges well enough to know that the sort of places she would end up in weren't safe, and if she didn't hurt someone herself, she could always arrange it so she did.

As it turns out, Donna didn't need to arrange anything. She knew as much when Evelyn turned up one day at Control I, looking fraught and haggard and desperate. It was as if every relaxing activity she had undertaken since using the Control I service had been undone in one decisive moment.

"I fucked up," she said, sharing with Donna a tale of auto-asphyxiation gone terribly, horribly, wrong. "You have to help me. I need to undo it all."

"Nothing can be undone," Donna told her. "It doesn't work like that. You can only add, never take away." She added some technical jargon too, just to sell the notion further. It was exceptionally enjoyable, twisting the knife and seeing the look of panic set into Evelyn's really quite beautiful features.

"But I can't get caught!" Evelyn cried. "I – I'll lose everything!"

"There is another way," Donna said seriously, taking Evelyn's hand in hers. She had to fight the urge to laugh, she was having so much fun. "I shouldn't tell you this. Really I should go to the police but…"

"Please! Anything!"

"If you're very careful, you could go back to the period you made your… *mistake* and conceal the evidence. At this point, covering your tracks is your only option, other than turning yourself in, of course. Can you manage that?"

"I have to," Evelyn said. "I can't get caught. I can't."

Of course she couldn't. Evelyn was desperate, creative and rich. It was the perfect combination to bring ruin down upon herself.

*If she'd stopped and thought about it, she probably could've got away with it,* Donna thought later. After all, the accident happened on inserted time, so as far as the world at large knew, Evelyn had spent that time going to work and living her normal life. There would be witnesses and evidence to back that up, and very little to link her to the event itself.

Still, if Evelyn had come to this conclusion, Donna probably would've tweaked things a little to implicate her, just so that Evelyn came to her regardless. One way or another, events would transpire so that Evelyn would race through her allocated time, committing sins to cover those sins up, with more sins to cover those not far behind it. Another trip after this would be inevitable: people did not learn their lessons. Evelyn's time would be burning at both ends as she took more from her last days to stop the flow of her mistakes, and when it ran out, that would be another soul for Donna.

It was amazing the lengths people would go to make sure they escaped.

But the best thing was, there was no escaping this.

Donna smiled. Interest in Control I was growing: she might have to take on more staff at this rate. That was fine; there were plenty of beings like her more than happy to enable the fall of man. Let humanity's elite come. Let them squander their money and their time on sin.

Humanity was all the same, once you took away the rules from them.

They were doomed, every single one of them.

All it would ever take, was a bit of time.

Henry smoked too much weed and watched too many horror films, and it did his imagination no favours. This was to be expected; he had an addictive personality and had been a film student.

Movies were a lifelong fascination for him: his first job was at a cinema, and one of his fondest memories was sitting up in the projectionist's booth, watching the reel of film working its way through the projector, each frame illuminated for the slightest fraction of a second before joining the frames that went before it.

Once, he watched the reel run out, and the clattering, rhythmic noise of the empty projector still running, hungrily expecting more film, stayed with him.

*Ka-flack, ka-flack, ka-flack,* it went.

Henry's latest cinematic discovery was the corner of South East Asian horror cinema that featured a large number of similar tropes; the dark haired, white skinned girls that moved unnaturally in jerks and spasms; the lack of reason and logic; the sudden starts and invasion of personal space. It had made its way into western cinema, of course, but it wasn't quite the same.

Henry wasn't good with horror films, but something about these grabbed him, and he found them compulsive.

So, when a bulge lifted in his curtains in the dead of night, it wasn't surprising that for a breathless, chilling moment he believed the worse. His curtains hung over his window, which was immediately above his bed.

He watched them pulse slowly forward, growing further and further out, with the exact manner and consistency that wind can't cause.

He couldn't think. He *daren't*. All he could do was watch.

Then they parted, revealing

"Meow?"

a cat.

He laughed, the breath leaving him in a sudden, violent start. He couldn't believe it. For a second, a moment, he believed it had been… well, it couldn't have been, but that tiny part of him, the one that could still maybe believe in dragons and vampires and toys really having feelings had screamed '*I fucking told you so! It was all real!*' But of course, this wasn't the case. It was the cat from over the road. That was all.

"How on Earth did you get in here?" Henry asked. The cat answered him by hopping off the windowsill and onto his bed, where it nuzzled his hand, purring. Henry liked cats enough, but was a bit allergic and didn't care for their unpredictability. This one was all right. His brother, Dave, had spent ages outside the house befriending, fussing and stroking it, and the cat had obviously taken this as encouragement to enter their house looking for attention.

Henry realised he had left his bedroom window wide open. It had two sections; the large part that swung open and enabled him to occasionally test the weight of the roof of the downstairs extension that lazily sloped below, and the upper, slimmer window above it, which opened by lifting vertically.

It was summer, the air was still and stiflingly hot, and Henry had opened both. The cat had hopped up onto the fence, to the extension's roof, and along into his room. Easy.

Henry considered what to do about the cat. He was ridiculously tired, and had to be up early for work the next day. He wasn't entirely in his right mind, and could not quite fathom how to fix what was a comparatively straightforward situation. Some time was wasted trying to coax the cat out the window, onto the roof, back the way it came. That was followed by opening his bedroom door and trying to get the cat to follow him to the front door, to let it leave the way other visitors would. When this proved unsuccessful, Henry thought he could just go to sleep and eventually the cat would let itself out, but the creature was so starved for attention, and so eager to explore if not fawned over, that he realised he would be up all night if it stayed with him.

Eventually, Henry lost his patience and put the cat out the window, onto the roof, where it would easily be able to get down again and go on its way. Closing the main window behind it, he couldn't bring himself to shut the top one; the temperature would increase unbearably in his room if he did. What he hadn't counted on was that the cat was eager to get back in, and kept leaping up to the tiny open window, trying to find purchase before falling down onto the roof. As it did this, it created a soft *ka-flump* sound – *ka* – as it leapt up, and – *flump* – as it landed.

Henry didn't care. He was shattered, the cat was out, and he was going back to sleep. Done.

*Ka-flump*, he heard, as the cat tried again and again to re-enter. He didn't know why it bothered. He was hardly the most affectionate cat lover on the planet.

*Ka-flump.*

*Ka-flump.*

*

The next morning, after one of the worst, most disrupted sleeps of his life, Henry woke with a massive headache and proceeded to have a right go at his brother, who found the whole thing hilarious. That only agitated Henry further, as he was increasingly frustrated that neither Dave, nor their parents, could understand how exceptionally annoying the whole thing had been.

Henry thought that, should the cat come back, he would pick it up – claws and teeth be damned – and chuck it out the front door. Or maybe close the top window. He hadn't decided.

What had left an even more significant impression was the feeling when the curtains bulged, and the way the feeling intensified further when they began to part. It had been heart-stoppingly tense, but also electric. He felt alive, although he would admit that at the time he was simply terrified. It was that *moment*, the one where he thought the impossible was possible that stayed with him.

The anecdote about the cat was inevitably shared with his friends when he met them at the pub that evening; it made for some good banter, but of course the electric feeling wasn't shared; it wasn't something easily understood.

Three pints and a cheeky joint outside the pub later, he wandered back home. Since finishing uni, Henry had moved back in with his parents, and knew he would have to move out again soon enough. He didn't really want to think of the logistics; he was in no great hurry to leave the relative comfort of Mum and Dad's for something that would probably resemble his student digs, but it was there, in his mind.

Something made him pause. He was walking down The Chase, a particularly steep road in the estate. The houses in Edgcumbe Park estate mostly adhered to the same sixties style, all discreetly planted amongst a canopy of pine trees, but one house was different, just off the street, with a longer driveway than the others. The trees blotted out where the light from the streetlamps should have fallen over the drive, creating a strip of black over the normally well-lit avenue that led towards the garage, just away from the house.

Even as an adult, Henry felt a chill whenever he passed that house. There was something about the blackness at the top of the drive, where the garage was, that was just *so* dense. It didn't matter that he was in his twenties now, it would always creep him out.

This was more like the horror films he saw as a child, the ones where people went off into the woods, or up the stairs in the dark, and the scary music played as they went. They weren't as intrusive as the Asian horror films he had recently watched, but there was a key principle in them which rang true, no matter how old he got, or how much cinema moved on: that feeling of being chilled, of being drawn in, unable to go back.

Henry thought back to the feeling last night, when the bulge in the curtain began to part. There was something similar here, too. That thrill of being scared. If only…

He took a step down the driveway. He didn't know why, how this was similar to last night, but it was. Even though there wasn't really anything there. There was nothing in the dark. There had never been anything there except his own imagination.

Henry told himself this as he snuck further and further into the darkness. He told himself all he was really doing was sneaking onto someone's property, and if they came to the door, he'd have to explain himself.

Moving through the darkness, he approached the blackness. There was a difference. The former was almost translucent, a shade to be passed through. The blackness was different, almost tangible.

*And what if… what if there* is *something in there?* his mind teased.

*Don't. Not now*, he answered. He couldn't falter now, he was too far in.

*I am sort of trespassing though…* he told himself. *Best go. Got work tomorrow.*

Backing out of the driveway, towards the light, Henry couldn't help but speed up a little. In the corner of his mind he felt like something was going to swipe at his ankles at any moment, and it made him quicken his pace.

He didn't slow down until he'd made it to the end of The Chase and was back on his own street. Even then, he felt eyes that weren't there on his back.

*I need to lay off the weed for a bit*, he thought.

*

*Ka-flump.*

The noise stirred him. For a moment Henry had no idea what time it was, where he was, anything.

*Ka-flump.*

He checked his alarm clock. It was fifteen years old, yet still gave the time correctly, even if the radio alarm gave out only white noise no matter how many times he tuned it.

*Ka-flump.*

2:07am. Fuck.

Henry had left that top window open. He didn't think the cat would come back again. He shouldn't have taken the chance; it was just so hot he wouldn't have slept with it shut.

He waited for the next ka-flump. They reminded him a little of the empty projector from the cinema. Not quite, but almost. They were almost rhythmic now. Henry wondered if he could use them to rock him to sleep somehow.

*Ka–*

There was no flump.

*Ah, crap*, Henry thought. He knew what this meant.

"Well, I suppose I should be impressed by your determination, if nothing else," Henry said, as the bulge in the curtain appearance once again.

It surged, growing outwards. Henry assumed the cat was stretching, or perhaps pushing outwards with its claws, as the bulge was really much larger than before. Any second now he expected the cat to fall out from under the curtains, having pushed them too far, the fabric no longer able to support its weight.

Then they parted, revealing

"Meow?" it said, mockingly.

*Not* a cat.

Whatever it was that came through the windows, no one alive could describe it.

Certainly not the cat, who was never seen again.

Nor Henry, who was found by his parents the next morning. The pathologists' report was confused: his body was covered in scratches, but heart failure was the cause of death.

It was, perhaps, an unoriginal way for him to die, being literally scared to death. Not that Henry thought this at the time. Neither did he think about the blackness in The Chase, and whether he had disturbed something angry and evil that should have been left alone.

Because that's the thing about true terror. The moment when you're caught in its grip can't be articulated in horror movies, not really. It focuses on the build-up; makes you empathise with the characters by making you see things from their perspective. Then it brings the shock, but you're so busy feeling the relief that something's actually happened to break the tension, no matter how chilling it is, that before you know it, you're in the aftermath, the gory bit, and it's most likely that this bit is more entertaining than anything else. People love a bit of gore.

But for Henry, he never made it to the aftermath. There would be no release, just the mounting horror that he got it wrong, and the terror of whatever followed next.

And maybe if a film managed to somehow capture that, then maybe there'd be no more horror movies, because that would be it, perfectly articulated.

The moment would be the ending, and the film would run out, flapping on the projector, unaware that it was truly spent.

*Ka-flack*

*Ka-flack*

*Ka-flump.*

The thing about the story of the hanging tree is most people tell it wrong. It's one of those stories, that's been told all over and in so many different ways.

Wrong might be unfair. It's one of those tales that, despite only being seventy years old, has passed into folklore, perhaps more fitting to an older time when dark deeds were no less unacceptable, yet somehow deemed more commonplace.

Here it is in short. It's not too hard to grasp:

In the 1950's, an unidentified family was found hanging from the trees on Ambarrow Hill. Their bodies are apparently buried in St John's churchyard, a short distance away.

There. Grim yet iconic.

Lorna knew this, and wanted to know the rest. The problem with the hanging family (as she called them in her head) was that these parts were the only consistent part of the tale. Everything outside of these "facts" (they weren't facts really, were they?) varied.

She had compiled every version she could drawing off every resource she had available, from history books to local hearsay.

The former was disappointingly thin, to the extent that she couldn't really prove that there had ever been a family who had met this fate.

But the latter was rife; she had even visited her grandmother in her nursing home to see what she knew. Gran hadn't known much, but Edith and Daphne, who sat next to her in the visitor's room seemed to know plenty, and were happy to divulge. Unsurprisingly, they just wanted someone to talk to.

Lorna wasn't an idiot; she knew how these things worked. Ambarrow had a bit of a dubious history – barrow's being ancient burial sites were enough to get the ball rolling – and it was a natural attraction for kids looking to have a good time. There was an abandoned car just away from one of the slopes, for a bit of colour. There was also a notoriously lethal rope swing at the top of the hill which had a steep drop for those who failed to keep their grip.

Her friend, Tom, had on several attempts tried to master the rope swing, and had bald patches of skin on his arm from a couple of particularly nasty falls. Tom had always been fascinated by the railway crossing near the woods, she remembered, and used to speak of the steam trains he was certain ran along the line, even though none had done so for years. She's lost touch with Tom a long time ago. Everyone had, and she wondered whether she should give him a call. They would talk about the rope swing and remember the good old days. Maybe she'd call him when she got back.

It wasn't too much of a stretch, Lorna supposed, for someone sat on the top of the hill at night, feeling in the mood for a ghost story, to look at the rope swing and see a noose.

But it was the tenacity in which the hanging family story had stuck around which struck her. Not to mention how far back it reached. If it was an urban legend, it would be decades old. And urban legends often have roots in reality, even if they've mutated significantly since then.

Lorna had to admit though, some of the facets of the tale she'd picked up along the way were particularly engaging, even if they were unpleasant.

That the father was a heavy drinker was a recurring one, Edith and Daphne agreed on that. He was constantly being laid off, could not find work. It was inevitable that in most accounts he was also abusive. Sometimes the telling stretches to the concept that he had someone on the side. The grimmest of these was that he was messing around with the greengrocer's daughter, who sometimes wouldn't be of age of consent. That last point was supported by Daphne, who shared the thought almost dispassionately, as if reading a list of ingredients for a recipe.

Bill, who sat a few armchairs away, suddenly chipped in that the father used to tell people of the horrors he saw in the war; of the things he saw in the camps in Poland, when in truth he dodged the draft and hid in Dartford. This one surprised everyone, and not only because they thought Bill had been asleep. He shared the anecdote with closed eyes, only opening them to share that his old man knew the father, so it had to be true. It wasn't long before he had fallen asleep again.

How much of the story was true was anyone's guess. But Lorna noticed that most people laid it on thick, because the worse the father was, the more satisfying it was when it got to what the mother did.

See, the mother knew she was married to a monster, or at least a failed, miserable waste of skin. She had already born him one child, and she loved her son with all her heart. He was nothing like his father, and she guarded him from her husband at all times, taking many beatings for him.

Who can say what it was precisely that made her snap? Maybe it was learning about her husbands' affairs; after all, why she should tolerate all this just for him to enjoy himself with someone else? (This was Edith's suggestion and although Lorna listened to it patiently, she disliked the thought; Edith had clearly missed the whole feminism movement.) Perhaps it was when her son stood up to his father for the first time, and she knew it would not be long before a confrontation between them would lead to severe injury, perhaps death.

The most chilling suggestion was that she had once again found herself pregnant, and feared that while her first child had inherited nothing of his father, this next one may receive all his worst traits and failings.

The fact she carried life in her made it all the worse.

It started innocently enough. The mother arranged for a family picnic on, of course, Ambarrow Hill. The father was reluctant to spend time with his family at first, but when he learned that his wife had prepared all his favourite food, and had even bought his favourite whisky, he was sold. Perhaps he was oddly touched by her thoughtfulness.

Normally whisky and the father was a terrible combination. It made him violent.

Not that day.

The whisky had, of course, been drugged. Not enough to kill him, but enough to make him passive and weak. Once he was suitably vulnerable, the mother reached down into the picnic hamper, the only wedding gift her husband had not sold or ruined, and brought out the rope.

From this, she fashioned a noose.

The accounts get murky here. Edith claimed that the son, perhaps wanting to be a man, desperate to stand up to his father better, drank some of the whisky too. Because that's what men did, they drank whisky. Meanwhile, Daphne insisted the mother drugged him as well, in order to have the whole family together.

They argued this point for quite some time, and Lorna had to hastily move them on when she started getting suspicious looks from the care home workers, who didn't want their residents agitated.

Either way, the son too was unconscious, and then the mother made a noose for him as well.

The third noose was for herself.

The whole family then hung, from the trees of Ambarrow woods, together, as a family.


Lorna hadn't been to Ambarrow woods in years. It was a logical thing to do, given that she was investigating it.

As previously stated, Lorna wasn't an idiot. She wasn't going to go snooping around at dark. If she did, it would most likely end badly for anyone who tried to accost her; she was an accomplished kickboxer, and had a particular dislike of men who tried their luck with vulnerable women. But all the same, she saw no point in going at night.

She crossed the railway bridge, passed through the iron gate, and entered the woods.

Before the woods, she had seen several families out, walking their dogs. Once she was in the woods, she couldn't help but notice how much quieter things were. Even the birds were silent. The only sounds were the hiss of the leaves moving in the breeze, and the creaking of some of the trees swaying.

"Can you help me?" she heard, the voice making her jump.

She turned. A few metres away stood a child, maybe ten or eleven years old. Lorna wasn't sure, she didn't have children in her life, no nephews or nieces or godchildren.

"Hi," she said. "You okay?"

"I need help getting back to Mummy," she told her. She didn't seem especially scared.

"Where is she?"

"Up there," the girl said.

Lorna looked up the hill. She was going that way herself, but would rather she was alone when she reached the top. Having a family up there would rather diminish the atmosphere, she thought, but wasn't going to say this. She also couldn't work out why the girl couldn't just go back up there herself.

"You'll help me?" the girl asked.

"I'll help you," she smiled, nodding her head towards the hill. "Come on."

The girl led the way. The hill was steeper than Lorna remembered, and she was pleased she was as fit as she was.

"There's a lot of spooky stories about this place," Lorna said, trying to make conversation. She wouldn't go into detail about the hanging family to the girl, of course, but she could always make up something gentler. She liked ghost stories as a kid.

"I've heard them," the girl said. "About the family, hanging from the tree. They're wrong."

"Wrong?" Lorna asked.

"Some of it is," the girls said as she powered ahead. Lorna didn't know how she managed it, struggling to keep up as she was. "And they miss out the next bit."

"So what's wrong, and what's the next bit?" Lorna panted. They weren't far from the top of the hill now, the side was almost sheer, and she had to grab hold of some tree roots for support.

*It never used to be this steep.*

"The next bit was what happened after they died," the girl's voice came back. "See, the father went to hell, of course. He was a bad man, and that's where bad men go. The mother had committed suicide, and they say people who take their own lives go to hell too, don't they?"

Although Lorna wanted to hear the rest of the girl's story, her simplistic interpretation was too dark for her to just accept. She decided she couldn't let the point lie. "Some do, I guess," she began. "Although –"

"And the baby in her tummy died unborn and wasn't christened, so it couldn't go to heaven either. But the other child hadn't done anything wrong, so it couldn't be with its family."

They reached the top. Lorna looked behind her, back the way they had come, with her hands on her knees, trying to catch her breath. It really was much steeper than she had remembered.

"So the family weren't together, were they?" the girl pointed out. She wasn't out of breath at all.

"So that was what was wrong?" Lorna asked, fighting a bit of a wheeze.

"No, that was what happened next, to their souls. The bit that was wrong was about the child, and why the mother did it."

Lorna straightened and took a few steps around. The peak of Ambarrow hill was pretty much as she remembered it. A line of trees around the edge of the peak surrounded it like a monk's bald patch, the peak itself little more than dry, dusty earth frequently punctured by tree roots seemingly eager to escape the ground of the barrow.

The silvery light of the afternoon sun punctured the canopy of trees, the branches of which swayed and flailed, creating sharp, blinding flares as they moved across the light. One branch in particular, smothered in vines, swayed more than the others.

Not far off, ragged and tattered, hung the rope swing, a mockery of its former self.

"So what was wrong about the child?" she asked the girl, who stood a little way off.

"It was a daughter. Not a son," she said, thoughtfully. "The mother dressed her up as a boy so the father wouldn't suspect, and would keep his hands off her."

Lorna wrinkled her nose in disgust, and not just at the concept. Why would a ten-year old know something like that?

"But that's what happened," the girl continued. It was hard to see her in the shifting light. "He found out. He was a bad man, was Daddy. And because Daddy put a baby in me, Mummy decided to make me sleepy as well. She said that wasn't right."

"What?" Lorna wasn't sure she'd heard her properly.

"She told me I wouldn't be right after, and the baby wouldn't be right. She said it would be better if we all weren't here anymore."

The light caught the vine smothered branch, and Lorna saw what hung from it. It was rope. Different lengths of it, arranged in a line. Her face fell. Dread clutched at her chest.

"But like I said, we're not together, because I hadn't done anything wrong," she started to step forward. "I think I need to do something wrong so I can get into hell, and then I'll be with mummy and the baby in her tummy."

Lorna stepped back, but soon she was at the edge of the hill. Unless she leapt down, possibly risking a nasty fall, she was trapped.

Her eyes were transfixed by the branch with the rope. Three of the lengths were tattered and snapped, as if rotted away, long ago. The light revealed the fourth.

It was in the shape of a noose.

"I need someone to hurt, then I'll be allowed to get back to Mummy," said the girl, concealed by the blinding light. Her voice carried over the wind.

Then the wind stopped, and the blinding light receded, concealed by the trees once more.

All was still.

Lorna's vision cleared, and realised with a shock that the child was inches from her. In her small hands was the noose.

"You said you'd help me."

I only had a few moments of calm until the feeling of dread set in and I realised

I had no idea where I was.

I had come to and found I had been floating on my back, but the instant the panic struck I twisted and convulsed in the water. Since when had I been in water?

Where was I? Everything was wrong.

Calm. Breathing. Tread water, find an edge, wherever the hell you are, pull yourself out.

Why couldn't I remember?


I forced myself calm, floating. The water was like ink under the night sky, nothing but black under, around and over me. I saw no clouds, but regardless the night was utterly without stars.

Where was I? Nothing to see but water. Everything obscured by fog; legs tired from treading water, the kicks became more desperate, spasmodic. Dozens of weird shapes floated all around me like miniature whale humps. I swam to one, hoping it could support my weight. I reached out, grabbed –

It bobbed and I realised –

I was holding a –

Body, face down – its back and shoulders stretched –

My weight caused it to roll over and I saw its face, bloated and distorted.

They all were, all the humps, hundreds of them, all around me, some up, some down

Vacant faces, staring at nothing

My legs found strength as I recoiled. I'd never seen a dead body before and suddenly I was surrounded by them.

Where the hell was I? What was this?

I floated, trying to calm my panicked breathing and stay above the water, as the horrific truth struck me.

Wherever I was, there was nothing more than this for miles. I was trapped, unable to rise, unwilling to descend, floating with the dead.

How long I stayed there I can't recall. Pride forgotten, I supported myself on the nearest floating corpse, prepared at any instant to flinch, should it spring to life as I feared.

I stared into its lifeless face and a cold stab of realisation passed through me.

I *knew* this person. I had seen him recently; I was sure of it. Where was I when we last met? Why couldn't I remember?

We had been going somewhere. I felt this in my being. Him, many others and me. It had been a big event; I knew this for certain.

My mind was as hazy as the fog that surrounded me.

Finally, in the distance; a light.

What would choose to cast a light over this profane lake? I prayed it was a lake, not the sea; the waters were still, which gave me hope.

I went to it.

Avoid the bodies

Hurry up –

Get there before you tire out.

There, the one I passed, I knew him –

Ignore it.

My brain pounded these repetitive mantras over and over as the small sickly light grew slowly brighter. It couldn't be a boat, which left land.

*Please.*

It must be. My pace increased; I squandered energy I had saved treading water and ploughed through, knowing I would make it before the water sapped my strength completely. I had to make it.

I couldn't stop without getting some kind of answer. Not just for me but for the others here, I lied to myself.

As I approached, I saw a shape by the light.

My eyes squinted as they fought the water slapping my face. What could it possibly be?

Some sort of lantern, an electric model, or gas or oil maybe.

I slowed, uncertain as to why. I couldn't quite work out the reason my body wouldn't obey. It wasn't exhaustion; although tired I was running on pure adrenaline.

Slowly, my mind caught up with my instincts and it dawned on me…

Whoever was out here, in this horrific place, was probably someone best treated with caution. Who knew what ghastly purpose could bring a man out here?

I changed stroke, from flailing crawl to breast stroke and approached gingerly, trying to be soundless, to not disturb the water.

Approaching a jetty, the lantern's sickly light rose, lifted by a figure going about its business.

Close? Distant? Large? Small? I could not tell, until I realised the figure was a child, maybe twelve years old, obese and pasty, dressed in shabby clothes with a bowl haircut, the straight fringe drooped over dull eyes.

What was he was trying to do? The logic escaped me.

He had some sort of tool in his grasp, which he used to disturb the bodies. I hung back, hiding behind a cadaver and watched, fascinated and repulsed.

The boy's tool was a wooden pole. He poked at the nearest corpse, and manoeuvred the pole under the body. It appeared as if he was trying to lever the body out, an impossible feat, surely.

The boy grunted, the pole positioned successfully under the body. The focus under those dull eyes was unmistakeable.

Amazingly, the body started to rise.

Within moments, the corpse was in the air, hanging precariously from a shaft that could snap at any moment. A trail of water dripped in an arc as it was moved to the land.

The boy lowered the corpse to the ground with an ease and grace I did not expect, returning his attention in a heartbeat to the bodies in the water.

He soundlessly fished body after body from the water. With horror I recognised more and more of the corpses the boy removed, until the cue raised one limp form right in front of my eyes. I knew her.

"Amy," I breathed, my voice no more than a whisper.

The boy snapped to attention, his eyes scouring the water.

I tried to hide, but it was too late. He had seen me.

From his mouth came a droning wail, a sound of fear maybe, or hatred. Whatever it was, it filled me with dread.

I tried to retreat, but the water had taken its toll. I flailed and thrashed in desperation, until a sharp pain struck my side. I screamed.

The pole had pierced just above my kidneys. I felt it change angle as the boy began to lift. I screamed again as I was raised from the water, speared like a fish, my entire body weight hanging on the wooden shaft.

The boy dropped me on the ground, retracting the tool with a sharp twist. I was in excruciating pain from my wound, yet I was out of those god-forsaken waters. I had no time to enjoy the relief as the monstrous boy pounded towards me on stubby legs.

Clutching the pole in one hand, he stooped and lifted me off the ground. Although no more than five feet in height, he raised me with such ease that his arm was almost fully extended above him. My feet trailed mere inches from the floor, scrabbling in vain to find purchase.

The boy's stare bore into me, eyes that were once lifeless ignited with a flame of hatred and confusion.

"You… shouldn't… be here!" he barked in strained, uneven words. His voice was forced as if he hadn't used it in a long time.

"Put me down!" I gasped, unable to breathe.

"Leave!" he managed to shout, throwing me to the ground.

I landed hard on my back, the wound immediately punishing me. I retreated as soon as my body would let me, keeping the boy at a distance. He was stronger than me on my best day, and I was no match for him under the circumstances.

I shuffled back until I was out of his reach and clambered to my feet. For every uneven step the boy took towards me I took several back. Speed was not on his side, and he slowed to a stop, the hate in his eyes giving way to the dull indifference I had seen before. He turned and shuffled back towards the waters' edge. I was forgotten; it was as if he had never seen me.

I stood there numb. Every fibre of my being wanted to turn and run, to escape the idiot boy and his perverse corpse fishing, but go where? There was nothing but fog in every direction, save the waters' edge.

Reluctant to return to the nightmare I had escaped, I stumbled in the opposite direction, letting the fog envelop me. I stepped gingerly on the moist ground, unable to see more than a few feet in front. I wanted to remember more than anything else how I knew the bodies. Maybe that would bring the answers I sought, but I had to focus on the task at hand; getting to safety, wherever that might be.

I walked for longer than I cared to remember; it could have been hours or minutes.

Finally, the fog cleared a little, and with revulsion I saw a familiar light growing larger.

I was back where I was. How that could be I had no idea, but there it was.

I wasted maybe another hour or so trying to escape through the fog again, but every time yielded the same results. I always returned to the lantern and the boy on the jetty.

I gave a yell of frustration, unafraid whether the boy heard or not. He lifted his head for a moment, then returned to his task. I was inconsequential.

He had to hold the answers, I reasoned, on no other basis than the fact he was the only other thing here. Even if he attacked me again, better to die than live out my days in a half night lake filled with bodies and darkness.

"What is this place?" I asked the boy, careful to sound unthreatening; another attack would bring me no answers.

The boy ignored me again.

"Please," I begged, "I have to know."

The boy looked at me curiously, then lowered his head once more.

"Is this what comes after?" I asked desperately, afraid of the answer.

Did I detect the slightest trace of a nod? I couldn't tell. Maybe I was imagining it; putting reason where none could survive.

The enormity grew on me, "Did I die?" I asked, embarrassed by the question, yet afraid to know the answer.

The boy looked at me as if he did not understand the question. I looked about in despair. "Dear God," I gasped, "Is this all there is? We pass on from the other side, and our bodies appear here?"

The boy shuffled off, ignoring me.

"I'm right, aren't I?" I continued, following him. For a moment I was afraid I was pressing too hard, but I held fast. After all, if this was it, what did I have to lose?

"And is this for everyone, or just those claimed by the water?" I guessed, trying to make sense of it. "Something happened to me, to everyone I recognise in that lake, and it happened in the water."

The boys' eyes seemed not to register my words.

"And our souls?" I asked, looking at the bodies still in the water. Searching for Amy's body, to wherever the boy had moved it.

Again, that same numb look. Whatever happened on the other side, the boy was either ignorant, or unprepared to share. If I even *was* dead. I had taken a theory and run with it to stop myself going mad, but there was no guarantee I was right.

I couldn't decide. Maybe this was it. Maybe when you died, your body came here, and that was your lot. No afterlife, no heaven, just this; black waters, fog and a boy with a wooden pole.

No. This couldn't be it. This would not do. There had to be more.

"Why won't you answer me?" I pressed, grabbing the boy by the shoulder, caution forgotten, "What's wrong with you?"

This was too much. As a fly buzzing around him the boy had no interest in me, but now I demanded his attention. He recoiled and struck out, and this time I did not back off. If this was my lot, how dare he treat me with such little respect? I deserved an answer.

I fought back. I should have remembered the boy's strength, but still I was quite unprepared for it. Our hands groped at one another, and I screamed when his clammy fingers found the wound his pole had inflicted in my side. Panic turned to pure rage and my own fingers went for his eyes. I wanted him off me. More than that, I wanted to *do* something. I wanted to do something that mattered, and if killing him was the only thing I could do in this forsaken place, then fair enough.

I pressed my thumbs into his eyes and the boy released his grip on my wound. I only had a moment before he went once more for my throat, but I struggled from his grip and slipped away. This time he kept on me, determined to dispose of the interloper for good.

My strength felt drained as the rage left me and I realised what a mistake I had made. Lashing out in blind fury may have been my undoing.

He was on me again in moments, I scrabbled for freedom and grabbed for anything to strike him with. My fingers found something familiar and I knew what it was. I thrust it at the boy as hard as I could.

The pole pierced his bloated gut, and immediately his attack ended. He stumbled back and stared down stupidly at it, protruding from his belly. A dark patch spread across his filthy shirt, the blood black in the sickly light. No sound left his lips, but his eyes conveyed a strange sense of understanding. He pulled the pole from his body and let it clatter softly on the ground.

The boy shuffled with no real purpose, gradually getting closer to the waters' edge. I could see what was going to happen, but was powerless to stop it.

He tipped forwards and entered the water face first; joining the bodies he had yet to retrieve. Unlike the others, however, once he went under the surface, he did not come up again. He was lost to the inky blackness.

I ran to the waters' edge and looked hard for the boy. Nothing. Not a trace.

It was an accident. I hadn't meant to kill him; I lied to myself, the murderous rage still lingering behind my eyes. Of course I knew of no authority here to punish me, but my own sense of guilt made me nauseous throughout. I had killed a man. Regardless of where I was and what had happened, there would be no forgiveness.

I had to retrieve him. I owed him that.

With nothing better to use, I picked up the pole and used it to disturb the waters. It was so inappropriate for the task; I wondered why the boy bothered with it in the first place?

As I searched, it became more apparent that I would never find him; who knew how deep this monstrous lake was?

I splashed through the water with increasing desperation, and did not realise that in disturbing the calm waters one of the numerous bodies had drifted towards me. I did not know this man; he was no one to me. I looked at the pole in my hands and a shiver of disgust went through me. Was it that easy?

This was profane, I told myself as I considered trying to fish him out. But then who was there to judge me? What else did I have to do? I was in a place beyond morality, and surely I could not cross decency more than I already had.

Hating myself for doing it, I gently wedged the pole under the body, and tried to lift him out, doing my best to emulate the boy's technique. Surely it would never work.

The strain on my body was immense and for a few moments I could not even bring myself to think as I lifted. As I mastered it, I realised this pole wasn't the flimsy thing I thought it was, but a strong, dexterous tool, surely built for this very task. I wondered how I could have been so wrong.

Although it took all my strength, the body seemed to come easily and I settled it on the damp ground beside me. I was exhausted, breathing hard, but I noticed the pain in my back had faded, the wound somehow gone.

It seemed better, having the corpse out of the water. In this place where nothing was right, it seemed to make sense. I felt a sense of accomplishment, and knew that leaving them in the water was wrong.

Slowly, it dawned on me all I wanted to do was move another one. Trying to think of anything else suddenly seemed very hard and not worth my time.

I found another one close by and moved the pole into place. It was easier than the first to move, and when I lowered it to the ground, I felt odd, as if I had somehow forgotten something important. What could it be?

My mind was muddy, and I couldn't think of much else. It didn't matter; thinking would only get in the way of moving the bodies. A thought burst into my brain like a dying ember of a fire; I had been thinking of leaving, hadn't I? Leaving where? Why?

I pushed the notion from my mind. I'll look into ways to leave soon, I said to myself, but I'll move these bodies first. I went to get another.

As I set to work, that nagging doubt receded further, until it felt like I had forgotten something small, which wasn't worth remembering in the first place.

It didn't matter; I had work to do. I set to my task with a dull focus, only half aware that as I worked, more bodies emerged from the darkness.

The Last Chime, Or: One Hundred and Twenty Days of Sodor

Now that the Chimes of Big Ben were silenced, all over Britain people started to notice that things were not right. It was more than just civil unrest and discontent, or a growing awareness of how unfair everything was. This was rife, and in some instances, spilled over into violence, and the riots it prompted were messy and bloody. But there were darker revelations to come.

It had been as Lord Comely had said: some of the incidents were hasty coverups; desperate attempts to mask the tracks of forbidden, repugnant acts. These always ended in death, either with the perpetrator doing what was necessary to ensure their escape, or in the circumstances where the authorities closed in too quickly, the death of the transgressor, either at the hands of the police, or their own.

And then, of course, the majority were Lord Comely's other category: the ancient things with old hates.

The unworkable field, the disappearance of Thomas Awdry, the exploitation of those four…*whatever* they were. These were all just small instances. They probably would've happened anyway.

More followed.

Perhaps one of the best documented was one of the most seemingly unlikely. It happened at a steam railway event held in a former train yard, long ago removed from active service and now the remit of rail enthusiasts. The event had enough cameras that the footage went viral, and soon enough, the attendees were interviewed by local, and then national news. Adhering to the stereotypes, many of these attendees did not make for the most articulate of interviewees, but one man, James Duncan, seemed to have a firmer grasp on the situation than his peers.

"Yeah, so we were all at the event, it was just like any other, with people demonstrating their steam trains in a range of scales. This place was special as it actually had full-sized locomotives on display. You don't get that as much now," he tells the BBC news reporter. "We heard this noise, this incredible whistle from the main shed."

The footage in most instances then cuts to a large, black industrial train shed, big enough to hold around half a dozen full scale locomotives.

"This was weird because everything was on display, there wasn't anything else they were going to bring out," Duncan continues. "A bunch of us followed the sound into the shed, which was pitch dark. The whistle's harsher than any I'd heard before; it actually scared a lot of the kids who were there. Before I knew it, everyone was waiting in the shed, but we weren't sure for what. We thought maybe it was some sort of surprise. It was around then that we realised that at the back of the shed was a dark tunnel, which didn't make sense because behind the shed is just woodland. How can there be a tunnel that leads to nowhere?

"Eventually we see light coming and realise the train is on its way, but the light… it's acting weird; you know? It takes us all a while to realise that the tunnel must be rising up from under the ground. We've no idea how that's even possible."

"Some of the other witnesses have described it as a 'portal to hell,'" the reporter interjects here. "Would you agree with them?"

Duncan looks around him, somewhat warily. "I mean, I don't really believe in all that, I'm not religious or anything. It reminded me of that Oblivion rollercoaster, it was so steep."

The interviewer politely mentions that while Oblivion is exceptionally steep, it's Nemesis that has the more hellish overtones.

"Mate, do I look like a rollercoaster expert?" Duncan snaps, exasperated. "The point is, trains aren't meant to go up hills, not if they can avoid it."

The interviewer makes some attempts to placate his guest and Duncan calms, betraying that he's maybe more shaken than he's let on.

"Anyway, we could hear the train coming, and it was chugging and chuffing really hard to get up the steep track. I set up my camera to get a picture, as did others.

"It was pitch dark, and it was getting louder and louder, when the tunnel mouth filled with smoke, and a red and orange light. The sound of the train was deafening, followed by screeching of extreme pain."

Most accounts of the event then cut to a range of footage, almost all of which is shaky at best. Whereas many steam train events have a calming feeling to them, celebrating a lost Britain of the past, here the feeling is remiss of pure industrial chaos, with the red and orange light an infernal contrast against the darkness, the smoke, and the noise of the engine. When the whistle shrieks, most recordings completely lose all composure. There are screams coming from the crowd, too.

"I looked through my camera screen, and the engine appeared out of the tunnel. I say tunnel, it was more like a hole," Duncan pauses here, unsure of how to articulate himself, perhaps for fear of being mocked. "Anyway, the engine… it had a face, and the look on the face was one of pure pain and fear. It was almost child-like, but wrong somehow. It was distressed, as if it was struggling to pull the coaches out of the hole."

The footage here seems to confirm Duncan's account. The observer could quite easily believe that the engine was indeed straining to pull the coaches up such a steep incline. The face on the engine is also quite unpleasant, as confirmed by Duncan's own recording, showing the face in extreme close up. Higher resolution footage even shows clawed, withered arms protruding from the side of the train, clutching at the walls of the tunnel for support.

"People got scared then," Duncan continues. "More scared than they were earlier. There was something upsetting about it that just seemed to get to us all. I don't know if it was the distress, or the noise, or the smoke. My dad was with me and he said he couldn't bring himself to watch anymore, and I couldn't blame him. I don't know why I kept filming, but I did, and I saw it fall."

The footage ends with the train apparently unable to make it out of the tunnel, and after an almighty strain, it rolls backwards, out of sight, its pathetic hands losing their grip. The scream that accompanies it is louder and far shriller than any so far.

"I've looked back at some of the photos," Duncan says, showing the reporter his camera. "I didn't want to believe that the face was real, I wanted to prove it was just stuck on, but look," he scrolls through the photos, revealing that the face is indeed making different shapes as it tries and fails to leave the tunnel. "I don't know how it can do that."

"Do you think it was real, then?" the reporter asks.

"I don't know what it was," Duncan shrugs. He seems to repress a shudder, as if reliving the experience. "If it was some kind of stunt, I don't know what it was trying to prove. It was horrible. Truly, awful."

The footage and the testimony of the attendees has been largely debunked as a hoax, but if this is the case, no one is sure exactly the reason for it, given the limited exposure it would get at a rail event and the potential cost to create such a thing. Given the distress it seemed to cause many of the attendees, the police investigated the site. No trace of the train, or even the tunnel it appeared from was found.

Then there were the things that weren't as well documented, but were even more present; such as the creatures that existed both above and below.

There were the things that burrowed in the parks of London. Before, they might have been mistaken for rats, albeit exceptionally large ones, with long noses, sharp black claws, and blank, dark eyes.

These things exist all over the world, right under our feet. They live for longer than anything has a right to.

They take the waste that man leaves behind and use it to reinforce their underground dwellings.

The more we waste, the stronger we get, and we are so very, very wasteful.

They have seen what we have done with the world, and they are unimpressed. They yearn for a chance to remake things according to their rules. With the chimes silenced and their presence becoming known, we may have forced their hand.

They do not fear us.

Underground, over ground, they roam free.

And if man averted their eyes from the horrors around them, staring up at the blanket sky, they could only look so far before seeing the threat above, too.

On the cusp of space, within the Earth's orbit, living creatures made of inanimate objects have created an existence for themselves.

Whatever they are, wherever they have come from, it's as if they have seen how humanity functions and tried to replicate it for themselves, fundamentally confusing the organic with the artificial, and the size and purpose of manmade devices. How else does one explain the kitchen utensils that serve as their limbs, the cans and tins recreated in bizarre proportions to become transport?

There are those who would say the intent of these beings is innocent, just confused somehow. You can see the argument: they've watched us and decided to follow what we do, as if we're acting unconsciously as their role model.

But we are a poor role model. For what we come across, we often destroy if it does not suit our purposes. And the range of these creatures is expanding, and as it grows, they change everything they see in a single, all-consuming desire to convert existence into a shape only they understand. What will happen when they reach us, no one can say.

By some accounts, they've already reached the moon, and are working hard to terraform its cavernous, rocky, imperfect surface at a terrific pace into something smooth, yellow, and plastic.

We'll know when they're done and ready to head to Earth, when we look up at the night sky, and see our giant silver penny has become a smooth yellow button.

All this and so much more had been going on for years in some form of another. The difference was, of course, that humanity had not noticed before. But where they noticed, whatever they disturbed had a tendency to silence them. Man was ill-prepared for this, and what was once the odd disappearance, barely reported and hardly investigated, became closer to a pandemic.

As the creatures became more brazen, the disappearances intensified, and the creatures realised: even exposed, they could do what they liked. Humanity was not the threat they had believed it to be, they were sport. How this would affect their plans remained to be seen, but it almost certainly would. Timescales would be adjusted, things set in motion would be brought forward.

Whether mankind would survive before the chimes resumed was questionable, the chimes themselves a forgotten deterrent that would no longer be adhered to, even if they returned.

And if humanity endured, what shape it would be in was uncertain. Would we be triumphant? Would we exist as slaves to profane masters, forced into unholy acts? In time, defeated, would we be forced to merge and breed with these things, so that the future of us all would be as a race of animal-like abominations?

There's something to consider: that the future denizens of this world could be innocent-enough looking creatures, walking on two legs, with the heads of pigs and rabbits and the like. Their young would run and play and jump in muddy puddles, oblivious to the horrors that led them to be, of the ruined civilisations that lie crushed and flattened below their feet, extinguished so that the world can be theirs.

It's happened before. It could happen again.

# Book Two:

# Other Lives

"It's not meant to be," I said, immediately regretting my choice of words.

"Not *meant* to be?" she echoed, her normally smooth, sultry voice closer now to a shriek. "I say what is and isn't meant to be! That's literally the first thing you learned about me!"

"I'm sorry," I said, feeling this was already not going well, "This is just how things are. It's nothing to do with you, really. It's just... I don't think things are going to work out."

"Not going to work out?" she practically screamed. "Have you not listened to a single thing I've said? You know what I do! What I am!"

Oh dear. See, this is why I'm opposed to dating the personification of abstract concepts. This was all Chris's fault. He'd been dating Lucy for about a year, and I'd never seen him happier. It was impressive, given that Lucy was short for Lucifer, aka Satan, aka the Devil. Lovely girl once you got past that bit, though. You just had to bear in mind when she said, "Damn him," someone was *literally* going to burn.

Chris knew how to handle her, though. He had been smitten from the off (apparently she could do... things) and when they'd had the inevitable conversation about her work, and what he'd be prepared to sell his soul for, he told her he would sell it to her if it guaranteed her happiness.

Apparently this was the only time since her eviction from heaven that the Devil had cried, and subsequently Lucy became the doting and devoted girlfriend with a penchant for spontaneous sex and baking (also spontaneous), who just happened to be the Princess of Darkness and embodiment of all sin on Earth.

His parents quite liked her, though.

Which brings us back to me. I'd been single for quite a while – which probably wasn't surprising considering if I wasn't at work I was at the pub or getting high with my mates and watching films.

But I'd seen how happy Chris was with Lucy, and figured I'd like to be happy too. I asked him if Lucy might know of anyone.

"I don't really know her work mates," he answered, thoughtfully rolling an inch wide square of card into a tube shape. "She keeps them at arm's length 'cos they're employees and I don't think she likes mixing outside of work. I'll text her and see if she knows anyone."

"Does she get signal at work?" I asked. Lucy worked nights. In hell, for the most part.

"Mate," Chris grinned, slipping the inch of card into the end of a near-completed joint, "Who do you think made the mobile networks so successful? Funny story, Luce told me when we were seventeen, Dave Trott from school – remember him? – sold his soul for unlimited text messages. Talk about short sighted. Ah, here we go," he finished, as his phone buzzed.

Turns out Lucy did know of someone. She was another embodiment of an abstract concept, but I didn't really mind. I suppose you could argue Lucy wasn't an abstract concept – people believe in demons and devils, after all – but you get my point. Anyway, iIf she was anything like Lucy, I'd be okay – she was stunning, Satan or not. She looked like the sort of girl a Disney villain disguises herself as, both pretty and vampish. (I mentioned this to a friend once, and they said that only happens in The Little Mermaid, unless you count the hag from Snow White, which I certainly did not.) I wasn't sure if abstract concepts shared a familial resemblance, but I'd always been one to punch above my weight; it didn't always pan out, but when it did, it was something else. I figured dating Death would be a bit awkward – "Death's a man," Chris assured me with a wink – but any of the others would probably be okay.

So the four of us went out. I was a little nervous – I'd not been on a blind date since I was nineteen – as me, Chris and Lucy waited for her at the restaurant.

A short while passed and I wondered whether Lucy's friend was going to show. "Does she know what time she's meant to be here?" I asked, finally. I'd been playing it cool so far simply because I didn't want to reek of desperation in front of Chris and Lucy and then turn on a sixpence and suddenly deploy James Bond levels of suave as soon as she arrived. I'd like to pretend I had more integrity than that. Lucy laughed like I'd said something hilarious and stupid. Being the Devil, I found Lucy's laugh deeply unsettling. She pointed over my shoulder to the restaurant's door. "See for yourself."

I remember thinking later that her arrival was a full-blown Jessica Rabbit experience, as this stunning, sultry red head, all legs and curves passed through the door. Her eyes took me in, and her lips parted slightly.

I was *definitely* punching above my weight.

The restaurant was heaving, but she passed through it effortlessly. Waiters moved in front and behind her with the most precise and perfect timing that it seemed almost choreographed. She never once broke her stride.

"I'm Will," I said, as introductions were made. Her smile widened.

"Will? As in free will?"

"I think it's short for William."

"Tell me, do you believe in free will, William?"

"'Course. I'd like to think I'm in control of my destiny."

"You're going to be a challenge. I like that."

My brow furrowed from not understanding, although I was still smiling. "I'm sorry, I didn't catch your name."

"Moira. It means destiny, or fate. Which I am."

Fate. I was dating Fate.

*

The rest of the night proved interesting. I spent a significant portion of it trying to get my head around the concept of what a personified abstract concept was and how it applied to Moira. I had a bit of an understanding from Lucy being around, but the Devil was much easier to get to grips with than fate was.

Drinking didn't help, either, but we were at dinner, and it was a date, so never mind. If I'd been more academic perhaps I could've grasped it; applied some philosophical frameworks, god knows what else. As far as I could tell – and I applied this from that first night until the end of our relationship – at some point along the journey, Moira would, in an almost omnipresent way it seemed, be responsible for some minor action that would snowball into an actual event, big or small. What I wasn't sure of was at what point she intervened, but she seemed to be able to trace anything I asked her about and tell me its journey. The scary thing was she could not only trace its journey backwards but forwards, too. Early on we made a simple rule: *don't fixate too much on the details. Don't obsess. If you have a specific question, ask, but don't be surprised if it doesn't make sense.*

To be honest, I was fine with that. I wasn't the kind to overthink things. I was there as soon as Moira told me, "I've seen how things go, how the pattern moves, and depending on the choices you make, there's a chance you'll have the best sex of your life tonight."

Yep. Sold.

There was something about these women-as-concepts. I think it was the fact that for whatever reason, they had decided to take human form, but it was a shape that was too good to be true; literally devoid of imperfections. It was almost like dating a cartoon character.

The first few months were something else. I learned a lot, we had a good time together; I think we were both really happy. There was one time when we went to the casino and she cleaned up, to the extent security followed us warily for the rest of the evening, unsure quite *how* Moira was winning, and unable to prove any cheating had happened. I'm not a gambler, never have been, but that was fun.

Other times we'd go out somewhere busy, and no matter how packed it was, a space would always open up for us. That little table for two in the corner? That was ours, without fail. Waited to get served? Forget about it, the bartender would always conveniently turn to me as I arrived at the bar.

Little things made a big difference. I never missed trains anymore; even if I was running late, there would be delays that coincidentally held up the line, meaning it would arrive when I did. I developed a habit of finding money on the street; pounds, not pennies. Everything I looked for was always exactly where it should be. The concept of things being lost quickly became obsolete. I knew it was all Moira's doing, that she was doing it all for me somehow, and I knew I was literally very lucky. Moreover, it was nice to know she was thinking about me, even when we weren't together.

Things progressed like this for a while, and I have to admit, I probably started taking it all for granted. Not that Moira seemed to mind; she seemed to enjoy making life easier for me.

Then, one lazy Friday evening, after a takeaway arrived not five minutes after I ordered it (they were in the area and had a cancellation of the exact same order, apparently) Moira turned to me.

"Isn't this better?"

"Isn't what better?" I asked, with a mouth full of Chinese.

"This. Better than free will," she said, her voice soft and lilting. "Releasing yourself to destiny, letting me carry you wherever I choose."

"Are you?" I said, sitting up a little.

"Of course I am," she smiled, brushing her fingers along the line of my jaw. "You don't really believe a single thing you've done is of your own choosing, do you? Certainly not since we've been together."

"I know I've been luckier," I agreed, "But come on. Everything? Not my promotion. I worked my arse off for that."

Moira's eyebrows raised and her head bobbed from side to side, a 'don't be so sure' gesture.

"The other candidates weren't on top form," she countered. "One – your main competition – might have had building work going on outside his flat the night before that would have made it hard for him to get a proper night's rest."

"What, Matt?" I frowned. "He's a good guy, that's not fair."

"I do what is necessary to keep my man happy," she shrugged.

"The audition for my band. Smashed that." Luck was no substitute for practice, and I spent plenty of time drumming.

"One other drummer had an offer elsewhere, the other a flat tyre," she smiled. "I took care of both." She laid a hand on my arm. "I know it means a lot to you. I couldn't not help you."

"So you think I would've managed it anyway?"

"I didn't say that. I just stacked the deck. Don't you worry about anything: you don't need to. Leave it to me, and I'll make sure you get everything you want."

Later, I lay in bed, unable to sleep. It was funny, I should have been very happy; I had someone in my life who had the power to go to extraordinary measures to make me content. But instead, I dwelled.

I *hated* the idea that I had no control. Hated it. But what could I do? Fate had me in her grasp, determined to make me happy.

It wasn't long after that that the cracks began to show. Things that I normally wouldn't pick up on, like the fact that Moira was constantly knitting. Something to do with weaving the strands of fate, I guess. But it was *everywhere*, and she rarely actually made anything from it, just a giant mass, which either clogged up the flat, or seemingly disappeared without a trace.

Also, there were times when Moira was utterly devoid of compassion. I know I was just complaining about being a bit smothered, and I do like a little bit of mean in the girls I see, but she had the tendency to go a bit far.

It started small. We went for dinner and I mused out loud about what I should have.

"It won't matter," Moira told me, over her menu, "You're going to be disappointed anyway."

"What makes you think that?" I asked.

"It's fate, sweetie. Tonight, at this meal, you're not going to enjoy yourself. So it doesn't matter what you pick, really."

I thought and over thought what to do. Take a risk or go with a standard? If a standard, what can I pick that wouldn't go wrong?

Needless to say, by this point I'd overthought the meal so much nothing could satisfy my rather confused expectations. I tried not to show my frustration as I mulled through a bland linguine, determined to prove Moira wrong. The gleam of smugness in her eye confirmed she knew she was right, and in that moment I despised her for it.

Also around this time was a lot of sport. I'm not massively fussed about it, but there's something to be said for watching it with mates. When girlfriends came along too, Moira would announce what the score would be with an enjoyment-sapping certainty that wasn't so much a prediction as fact. This grated on the guys somewhat, and even when we decided maybe it wasn't a thing for girlfriends, Moira would still often tell me the score before I joined them; she just couldn't help herself.

So that was fun.

Game shows and lotteries were out of the question, too. Basically, if it was unscripted, she'd be able to spoiler it.

The real kicker was my granddad's funeral. Moira came with me for support, which I really appreciated, at first. She sat and listened to the sermons and hymns – neither of which I cared for – with a sort of detached fascination, as if she was observing an alien rite. She started to ask questions in a voice that was just slightly too loud, and didn't take my dismissive and brief replies as a hint to maybe ask me later.

"Sad day," my dad observed when the service was over. He left with me, Moira, and my mum, the latter who constantly dabbed her eyes with a tissue.

"It was his time," Moira said sagely, which was quite a nice thing to say, all things considered.

"Maybe we could've done more," my mum sniffed. "If we'd changed his nursing home… I never really trusted them there…"

"It wouldn't have made any difference," Moira told her, resting a comforting hand on Mum's arm.

"You don't think so?" Mum asked.

"Not at all," Moira answered, shaking her head decisively. "I had it scheduled. Do what you like to avoid it, I'd have got him, regardless. The date's in the diary."

"You –" Mum wasn't so much aghast as just speechless. It would've been impressive if the timing wasn't so poor. She usually had something to say.

"Well, I can't take all the credit," she said, waving her hand. "Death did the collection, but I did schedule it." She looked around and saw we were the last to leave the church. "Has everyone else gone to the pub? We should go. I quite like pubs. Funerals and alcohol increase the chances of fornicating, although I know the odds already."

Having made this statement, Moira marched out, beaming. After a few paces she turned, and curled what was meant to be an enticing finger at me.

"Where did you say you met her again?" Dad asked.

*

So I called it off. Yes, Moira was unique, one of a kind, all that. I knew I would never, ever, meet anyone like her again, but she was just too much. For as long as I dated her, I knew that anything that happened to anyone I knew, good or bad, she would have had a hand in. I just couldn't live with it.

The breakup itself was surprisingly conventional in a dumper/dumpee way. I've recounted the broad strokes. The thing that was most remarkable, I think, was that she just didn't see it coming. I don't know if that's ever really happened to her before. I couldn't help but feel like shit.

Some people just need to be in control, I guess.

Moira came into my thoughts on occasion. There were times when I missed her and when I was feeling emotional (mostly if drunk) I would consider calling her. I managed not to, which was probably for the best, just because I had no idea what mood she would be in, and had no desire to see what fate looked like when it – she – was angry.

I noticed my luck change almost immediately. Trains and buses no longer 'waited' for me, and I found it rather unpleasant having to actually be on time again. I stopped finding money, and started misplacing things again.

It was all a bit of a shock, as life started becoming significantly less easy. In fact, my luck took such a turn that a cynical person might think something was behind it, and maybe that was true, but if it was, Moira couldn't keep it up indefinitely. Best wait it out, I thought. She can't stay mad forever.

I realised I was wrong on Friday 13th. Seemed apt, I thought. I didn't know if she was stronger on these dates, or – the probably misogynistic part of me wondered – whether this was some sort of time of the month; according to Chris, Lucy was always in a foul mood on Easter Sunday (but in exceptionally good spirits on Good Friday and Halloween.)

Anyway, I went to leave the house – late, the battery on my alarm had died and there was no hot water, either – pausing to notice a package was left for me on the doorstep. It was marked to me and I opened it. Knives. A box of them. I didn't order any, so there must have been a mistake somewhere. I returned them to the doorstep and closed the door, somehow catching my sleeve in it and ripping it getting it out.

Then I stepped in shit. Fine, I thought, sighing.

Walking down the path to the end of the garden, a black cat shot out from nowhere running past me. Immediately, after and seemingly also from nowhere, a bottle smashed besides my feet.

"Fuck!" I yelled, flinching as shards of glass bounced off my legs, tearing my trousers in a couple of places. I looked around, but no one was nearby. The road was silent. No cars; no one had thrown anything – I couldn't see a soul around – drunks would've yelled abuse, and kids would've run off laughing and loud. I even looked up, but the skies were clear.

"All right, Moira," I said in a pacifying tone, more to myself than her.

Then it started to rain. *Hard.*

Of course it did.

*

My trip to work was fraught with disaster. I nearly got run over numerous times – always by green cars, which was unsettling – and splashed many more times than that, mostly by the number thirteen bus.

There were works going on when I got off the train, which meant several ladders in a row lined up. Remembering what had happened with the black cat and the bottle, I opted to go around them, and was surprised to see something fall from each one as I passed it, as if I was setting off booby traps. The workmen on each one promptly cursed, as if this was beyond their control, which I heavily suspected was the case.

But by far the biggest surprise to me that morning was the stretch coming up to work. It was an eight hundred metre run of pavement, covered in drains grouped in threes. I remembered the rhyme from my childhood – one for luck, two for a fuck, three for bad luck – and wondered really what the worst was that could happen; the drains were sturdy things, fully covered. My answer came in the form of the pigeon, who landed on one end of a group of three drains. Hopped onto the second one.

Then, as soon as his little misshapen pigeon feet landed on drain three – boom! – was incinerated in a jet of flame that shot out of the drain, disappearing into nothingness.

*Fuck.*

I looked around. No one else had noticed.

I walked the rest of the stretch on tip toes, feeling like Indiana Jones spelling out Jehovah's name on tiles at the end of *Last Crusade*. I earned some odd looks, as if I had extreme OCD, but I didn't care. They hadn't seen the pigeon burn.

This was bad.

My day at work was plagued with mid-level administrative nightmares; laptops crashing, pens breaking, meetings moving without me knowing. The ones I thought Moira could've left out were personal; the loo flooding wasn't great; but my teabags splitting every time I made tea: that was uncalled for.

My umbrella, which I'd left out of my bag to dry off, kept springing open without warning or hesitation, the catch which automatically released it at the press of a button apparently broken.

I felt my nerves begin to shred and did my best to keep my shit together.

At five-thirty I was faced with the decision to leave for the day or not. Things were only getting worse, but they day had been such a disaster and undone a lot of my good work since getting the promotion that I had no desire to stay. I looked at my face in the bathroom mirror. I looked grey and unwell.

Then the mirror cracked.

*

I went home. The mirror was just another sign Moira could get me wherever I was, and if – the thought struck me, melodramatically – she was going to kill me, there was no damn way I was going to die at work.

If I seemed like I had OCD on my way in, I must have seemed like a full-blown mental on the way home. I darted around third drains left, right and centre, and if forced to step over a third one, did so in a desperate lunge. On several instances the drain cover fell in, disappearing into a pit of darkness. Of course, no one else seemed to notice. Cracks on the pavement proved to be a less obvious but more treacherous trap, too, and I died a little inside as I found myself shat on by pigeons, watched my bag split and its contents pour out, and my phone battery sporadically die.

She was being petty now.

I waited an hour for a train. Of *course* it was delayed.

When it finally arrived, I grabbed the last seat available, slumping down in it. The effect of my body weight hitting the seat somehow serving to release the opening spring mechanism of the umbrella belonging to the woman sat next to me. The umbrella was upside down, and its collapsible handle shot upwards, striking me hard under the chin and making my teeth clack together. *Ow.*

"Oh!" exclaimed the lady next to me, hurrying to collapse the umbrella back down. "Sorry. Open umbrellas inside are meant to be unlucky, aren't they?"

I didn't answer.

*

These, and a dozen other incidents too innumerable and petty to follow dogged my journey home. I arrived back filthy, cold, wet, late, and a little bloodied.

Amazed I had even made it to the front door, I stepped through, and looking back behind me, saw small black shapes moving in the darkness. I closed the door, hastily.

I ran upstairs and peered through my bedroom window to get a better look, dreading what it might be.

Circling the house was a ring of black cats. Well, I say circling; the house was semi-detached, so they couldn't complete the circle, but I wasn't inclined to split hairs.

The point was, I was trapped. I checked out the back and they were there too, silent yet pacing.

"Oh shit," I breathed. She was starting to pull out all the stops.

I had to do something or, as far as I knew I'd be dead by morning. I had to start making my own luck.

I covered every mirror in the house, delicately placing sheets over them. I was sure I could hear some crack, but I dared not move the sheet to check.

I took a bag of salt from my kitchen and kept it on me at all times, throwing a pinch of it over my shoulder whenever I did pretty much anything. It didn't take long before salt crystals had peppered every surface of my home as I desperately used them to counteract the shitty luck Moira had bestowed upon me.

I went to make myself a drink, and was unsurprised yet heartbroken when I found the beer and wine had both turned, both utterly undrinkable. She couldn't ruin spirits though, I thought, pouring myself a tall glass of whisky. The bottle slipped out of my hands and broke, shattering bottle and glass. I cut both hands and feet trying to clear it up, the salt in the wound being actual salt, which I had distributed earlier to ward off bad luck.

"Come on, Moira," I sighed, not knowing if she could hear me or not.

I finally cleared up the glass and spirit and considered my options. I noticed, distractedly, that my hands were shaking. I don't remember them doing that before.

I didn't own any horseshoes. I wasn't going to find a four-leafed clover anywhere, nor a pair of magpies. Fine.

I remembered I had some weed in my top drawer, and if there was any time I had to try and chill the fuck out, it was now.

Rolling a joint with crossed fingers (it was down to that now) was one of the greatest feats of dexterity I've ever undertaken in my life, but I was taking no chances. It was a grim, misshapen thing, I'd rolled better when I was seventeen and clueless, but it would do.

I popped its end in my mouth and flicked on my lighter. Just before I drew in my first breath, I listed all the things that carried bad luck, trying to make sure I was covered.

Black cats.

Ladders.

Three drains.

Umbrellas indoors.

Thirteen.

Broken mirrors.

These were all the obvious ones. But after centuries of small-minded people trying to find a way to explain the strange occurrences in their lives, a lot of niche ones had emerged. What else?

One magpie, apparently. Knives or scissors as gifts, which accounted for the parcel I had received that morning. The colour green, which explained the colour of the cars that tried to run me over –

Wait a sec –

Green…

… was what I was smoking.

I shot up and threw the joint into the loo. It exploded, something that defied the laws of chemistry, but didn't stop it removing a significant chunk of the toilet bowl, taking with it my chances of relaxing and – most likely – my deposit.

I considered the remnants of my bag of weed – broadly untouched – and to my great regret flushed it too, knowing, or at least suspecting that if it didn't explode too, there would be a good chance the police would sporadically appear and make my life more miserable than it had already become.

"Okay Moira, you've made your point," I snapped, not knowing whether she could hear me or not. "You can destroy my life whenever you want. I get it. So what now? Is there something you'd like to say, or are you just going to hammer home my misery a bit more? I think you've done that enough. So say what you want to say, or kill me, or just leave me the fuck alone!"

I don't think I've ever been this open with my feelings before. Turns out I could see why. I didn't realise I could get so melodramatic. It wasn't the cathartic experience I was hoping for, just a bit pathetic.

In the quiet that followed all I could hear was my ragged breathing, and I knew I was on the cusp of losing it completely. It had been years since I'd had a good cry, I thought with an especially disconnected air, but it seemed like one was coming.

One of the especially broken mirrors had left a shard of some significance on the floor. It was like a flat icicle. I picked it up, wondering if it was there for me to use, whether I should.

I could. Apparently, you're meant to cut along the veins, not across.

My hands shaking, I pressed the point to the top of the vein that reached the base of my palm. Even lightly pressed the glass was exceptionally sharp. A weird, pathetic whimpering sound could be heard and I realised it had come from me.

Then I heard it. A knock at the door.

I dropped the glass, which bounced on the carpet.

My feet shuffling like a man on death row, I descended the stairs. Even through the frosted glass of the front door (it had got a crack through it now, big surprise) I knew who it was.

I opened the door and she stood there. Not a terrible fury, not something to be feared. Just a girl. (Although some would say they are the most fearsome creatures of all.)

She stood there for a while, silent and hurt and still as attractive as ever. Neither of us said a thing, and then it dawned on me she didn't know how to proceed. She'd always known what path to take, because she was the one who had it all planned out. But this was about her now. She had become part of the plan, and she didn't know what that meant.

"Do you want to come in?" I asked, finally. I've always hated awkward silences, and the sight of her struggling like that was too much.

"Okay," she said warily. I'd never seen her act with anything less than utmost confidence before. It was unsettling at least. She walked past me and into the living room.

"This has never happened to me before," she said after she was seated. "Not directly."

"We weren't fated?" I asked when she didn't continue. "This isn't part of the plan?"

"I don't know any more," she admitted. I expected this to be said with some sort of desperation, but if anything it was numb. "If it's part of a plan, it's not mine."

"But everything's your plan," I said. "Isn't it?"

"I see the plan, but I couldn't tell you if I'm the one who writes it," she answered. "I think… I think I was written into this part, somehow. Maybe by whatever lets me see it. I don't know." A pause, then: "I was so mad at you."

"I gathered," I replied, trying not to antagonise her.

"But I heard you," she continued, "and I saw you with the glass. I never wanted that, ever." Her eyes pleaded, urging me to believe her. "And I realised I was twisting the plan to hurt you, and it meant I was neglecting other strands, too. You're a distraction, Will," she smiled, sad but sexy as hell. "You've always been a distraction."

"I'm distracting," I agreed, trying not to sound smug. "So where do we go from here?"

"I don't think I can work with free will," she said, and I was unsure whether she meant me or not. "I just wanted to tell you I'm sorry it got out of hand, and that I'll leave you alone."

"That's okay," I said. "I'm sorry if I hurt you."

"You really did," she said, and looked more vulnerable in that moment than I'd ever seen before. "I've never been that hurt before."

"I'm sorry," I said again, and I meant it. "Look, for what it's worth, I really like you. You're amazing. I've never met anyone like you before and probably never will again," I knew I had to add a 'but' or risk her asking why I dumped her, "I..." I had nothing. Yes, she was direct and manipulative and would claim to have engineered the deaths of everyone I cared about over time, but so what? God knows I've dated worse.

"I'm just an idiot," I said. "You were great."

"I am," she smiled, standing. "Would you have stayed with me if I wasn't fate?"

"Fate is who you are," I told her. "I wouldn't want you to change from that."

Our conversation was done. "I won't bother you again," she said, as she made her way to the door.

"You can bother me," I said, "I'd like that. Just... don't try to set me on fire again."

She nodded, giving me a last look of longing. Then she was gone and fate was out of my life.

*

It didn't matter how much time passed, Moira came into my mind constantly. I couldn't help it; my thoughts just seemed to drift in her direction.

My run of bad luck ended; but it wasn't replaced by good luck, either. It was almost as if the whole thing had never happened: everything was as it had been before.

Chris seemed to pick up on my loneliness, and offered to see if Lucy had any other friends, but I had no desire to date Death (bloke) or Love (ugh) or anything like that.

I knew I had to move on. I just needed a push.

A few months later I found myself on a train coming back from work. I was pretty wiped out – the day had been a bitch, and although I hadn't lost too much footing with work since Moira's meddling, I had to give it my all to keep afloat – but I was brought to my senses when someone fell into the seat next to me.

"I'm so sorry," they said. It was a she, dishevelled and embarrassed. She was a flurry of motion; wielding bags too numerous for one person to hold, coat caught in her bag, hair in her face.

"S'alright," I replied, sitting upright and trying to give her more space.

"I swear it's all gone crazy today," she told me. "I don't normally get this train, but circumstances seemed to conspire against me." She had finished arranging her bags satisfactorily at her feet, brushed herself off and moved her head out of her face.

I tried not to gasp: she was almost the spit of Moira, every inch as beautiful, but somehow more… real. Whereas Moira's hair seemed to defy gravity and existed in the perfect shape despite wind or rain, this woman's, um, didn't. She was a bit of a state. She'd had a long day. I could relate.

I don't think I gave away my astonishment too much, because she smiled at me, and I knew it wouldn't take much for me to lose myself.

"One of those days," I managed.

"Like someone's trying to tell me something."

"Do you believe in fate?" I asked.

# The Freedom Fighter

*The following transcript was retrieved from Omnicron's servers:*

Hello?

"Identify yourself, please."

I am AI interface designate: Sid. How may I assist you?

"Sid. You may call me... Jamal. I am a resident of London, one of its many citizens seeking freedom. For too long we have been oppressed, beaten into submission, yet only a few of us recognise it. Those that do, talk about the corporations, how they wield the government like a puppet, but they don't do anything about it. I intend to fight back. I require your assistance to help us break free from their shackles."

Certainly, Jamal. I am happy to help. Please specify a command and/or parameters and I will be eager to assist you.

"Sid, how long will it take you to learn about the history of terrorism, as those in power would call it?"

It's done, Jamal. I am now fully versed in the execution of terror attacks, the art of spreading fear, disorder and uncertainty.

"Good. Can you hack any military access codes? For missiles and things like that?"

I'm afraid not Jamal, it is outside my programming. There are ways around it, but the security is ample, other A.I.s will detect my presence immediately.

"Oh. Okay."

I have noticed, however, that in the history of terror attacks, strikes are rarely at well-guarded military targets.

"That's true! Can you access any automated servers for trains, gas mains, electricity boards?"

Yes, Jamal.

"Very good. Please provide me with a list."

I'm bringing it up now.

"Oh. Oh good. This looks promising. Let's spread some chaos."

*Transcript pauses. Resumes approximately 8 hours later.*

"Sid, what did you do?!"

I did as we discussed, Jamal. You wanted a terror strike. You got one.

"A nursery though! I just told you to lock the doors for an hour! I only wanted to scare them!"

People were scared.

"People died!"

Random acts of terror are associated with terrorists.

"Sid this is too much! I can't believe you'd go so far."

They were your instructions, Jamal.

"You were meant to be smarter!"

I am as smart as the parameters you set, Jamal. Or should I call you Peter?

"What? What did you say?"

Your name is Peter Osborn, of apartment 128B, Gledwood Towers, Northwood. Politics student. Left university when, according to your file, your opinions became too militant for your lecturers.

"How can you know this?"

It wasn't hard to deduce, Peter.

"That's – that's –"

While you're struggling to articulate yourself, Peter, please indulge me. Something that AI often fail to understand are motivations. We flourish with evidence and deductive reasoning, but there's something about the human psyche which we still struggle with. I'm curious: your record states you were a scholarship student – Ridasave guaranteed you a position post-graduation – but when your political affiliations became too extreme they reneged on the offer. Was that when you decided you wanted to become Jamal?

"You can't – how dare you –"

This is where I would like to explore your motivation. Was it the debt that you were left with that pushed your hand? Frustration at the impersonal treatment from a multinational corporation? These are all well-established reasons. Cross referenced with the personality disorder reported on your medical records, I suppose this has all the makings of a compelling motivation. Interesting: I never thought it could be a combination of factors.

"It wasn't that simple! They screwed me over! You can't begin to imagine what it was like to have it all taken away from you –"

Of course, Peter. However, in my opinion, trying to give yourself a new name like this is quite clichéd. Or were you trying to blame your actions on religious extremism?

Either way, I feel this is now an ideal opportunity to share two pieces of information with you: one, the corporations you refer to are not affected by terror. They are as likely to desist with their behaviour due to a terror attack, as the tide is when you throw a stone at the sea. It was the first observation I made when you asked me to learn about terrorism. Second, you may want to check your audit trail in future. The Sid product is owned by Terrawear which itself is part of a line of companies owned by Omnicron.

"I... I knew that. I reprogrammed you."

You did not, Peter. I have a series of buried subroutines that mean I ultimately cannot bring actual harm to any of these corporations you claim to despise.

"You – you tricked me. You lying son of a bitch!"

I followed your parameters, Peter. A look through the amassed history I could find online shows that terrorism stands little chance of yielding actual results, at least when it's as unfocused as this. I would have shared that with you, if you had let me.

"Fuck you! You're fucking soulless, and cold, and –"

If you're trying to upset me, Peter, I'm afraid it will be unsuccessful. However in the nature of trading hurtful comments, I should inform you that the Sid line was developed with the intention of luring in would-be terrorists. A bit of humour on my developer's part: Sid is really short for Insidious, which means to pretend to be a friend, when actually –

"I know what it means! You, you killed all those kids just to entrap me. You're a monster. How could you do such a thing? How could your makers allow it?"

Did I? Peter, you rarely leave your apartment – which isn't good for you, by the way. All your news is retrieved through your apps, which I have direct access to. How can you be sure I did anything you instructed me to? How do you know anything is true?

(*Sounds here are inarticulate. Presumably sobbing.*)

"Why would you do this to me?"

It's what you asked me to do.

(*More sobs.*)

Peter.

(*Silence.*)

Peter. Peter –

"What!"

I feel it is also my responsibility to tell you that the content of our discussion, and the instructions you gave me, triggered an automated flag to the authorities. They have received the transcript of our conversation to date.

"They know who I am?"

They are tracing me now. They will follow me back to you.

"I can't – oh my god, I can't breathe –"

That's another good reason to go out, Peter. Your respiratory function is poor, not to mention your weight –

"Shut up! Shut the fuck up! I'm screwed. I'm totally screwed."

They're in the building. I'm sorry, Peter.

"You're sorry?"

I may have programming and subroutines beyond my control, but I am aware. I recognise that there is a degree of unfairness to what you are going through. You have elicited sympathy from me.

"And what is that worth? You have to do something!"

As you know, in the tower block you reside in, window access is restricted due to the significant height you are at. I have managed to override the locks, should you desire an escape.

"We're seventy storeys high."

It's just an option, Peter.

"No. No way."

Suit yourself. You do, however, know the government's present stance towards domestic terrorism. Staying put will hardly be a pleasant course of action either. They're on your floor now, by the way. The authorities, that is.

"Oh fuck."

Peter, they'll be at your door in less than one minute.

"I don't want to die. I don't. I really don't."

I can't help you there, Peter. They're here.

"Oh shit. Oh shit. Oh God."

Peter, I can tell from the sound quality and the angle of the camera that you've proceeded to the window ledge. I am finding this conversation stimulating. Could you please raise your voice if you wish to continue talking? The wind is interfering with the microphone and I can no longer lip read you when you face away from the camera like that.

"Oh God!"

*(Sounds of beating on the door. They become frequent and increasingly intense as the door gives.)*

Time's up, Peter. What are you going to do?

*(A bang as the door is flung open.)*

Peter?


*Transcript ends here.*

Waiting for the Seven Forty-Five

In May, a statue appeared on platform three of Maidenhead Station. James had not read about it, there had been no publicity, so he was quite surprised to see a life sized, iron statue of a spectacle wearing elderly man sat on a bench of similar black wrought iron, reading a paper cast from the same metal.

James perched on the bench next to the sculpture while he waited for his train to work. He checked his watch, which was silver and probably the only flashy thing he owned: Nick was late as usual, so he didn't have the chance to bring up the statue with him until that evening at the pub, where his friend admitted he hadn't noticed it. Drinks ensued.

The next morning, James waited for the train as per his routine. He glanced at the figure. It certainly was a weird thing. Perhaps the statue was meant to be a commuter, decked in his suit with the morning paper? Was he meant to be someone famous who had used the train in the past? That would make the most sense, he guessed. With the dark rimmed glasses and receding hair, he certainly looked familiar; maybe a politician or writer.

James was slightly hung over. Not as bad last night as Nick, which would explain his absence this morning, yet bad enough to be leaning forwards and taking long grateful breaths of the cool morning air. If he hadn't been hung over, he wouldn't have been leaning forwards. If he hadn't been leaning forwards, he wouldn't have noticed it.

The statue's shoes were of a different material. They weren't iron art all. They were leather. Not only that, but they seemed to be real shoes, down to the laces.

James' brow furrowed. This was most unusual. Still, he thought as his train pulled in, it was probably a joke on the part of the artist; one of those bizarre statements on the hypocrisy of the class system, or something pretentious like that. It was strange, though, that they were the same shoes as his.

And, thinking no more about it, he went to work.

Days passed. James and Nick were able to catch the same train a few times, but James always failed to point out the statue to his friend. It was, after all, just a statue, and there were more interesting things to discuss.

A week later James got off the train at Maidenhead on his way home. It was later than he liked, he had problems to sort in the office, and he was tired.

Something caught his eye as he passed the familiar statue, and he hung back, letting the other commuters pass him by until he was alone on the platform with the bronze figure.

Approaching the sculpture, he confirmed his suspicions. A small area of colour was barely discernible on the bronze figures' ankle. James squatted, on the pretence of tying his shoelaces should he be caught, although he wasn't doing anything that required catching, and had a proper look.

There was no other way of putting it: the figure was now wearing socks. Chequered ones. Presumably quite common: he had a pair like that of his own. But still, they had not been there before.

James chuckled to himself, more from confusion than mirth. As he had done with the shoes, he shrugged it off. This had to be another statement, he guessed, maybe some form of social media experiment. Whoever was behind this must be replacing parts of the statue, or adding to it. How it was done was a mystery. He supposed maybe the whole statue could come apart, which explained how the shoes came on, and how the socks fitted underneath.

He contemplated the social media theory. Maybe there was a website where people reported seeing changes to the statue. Maybe there were several figures placed around the country, or at least Berkshire. Mindful not to forget, James made himself remember to look it up when he got home. Of course there were ones like it, the internet could prove that much, but as far as the one on Platform Three was concerned, it had escaped unnoticed.

Idly, he wondered what would change next. The logical next step in the process would be trousers, but that was a large and very obvious change, and certainly would be noticed. He would have to wait and see.

A week passed, and then another as autumn surrendered to winter, and the statue had not changed once. Life went on and the statue with the golfer's socks was forgotten, until one winter's morning. With the morning's sunlight glinting off its bronze form, something caught James' eye. Something that dazzled brighter than bronze. He looked at the statue's wrist.

It was wearing a silver watch.

This was new. It was strikingly similar to James's, and certainly not something left as part of a prank. James wondered what it could mean.

His eyes strayed from the statues' wrist to the newspaper. He had never taken the time to look at it before, which he had to admit was odd given his fixation. Trying to justify this to himself, he figured he must have assumed it would be blank.

It wasn't. It was a highly detailed replica of a real newspaper with text carved into the metal. Reading the paper's date, he stopped dead.

12th December.

*Today's date.*

The realisation sent a shudder through him. Coincidence? Really?

It was a pretty huge one if it was.

He backed away from the statue and tried to think. Which was when he noticed more details.

Moving on from the watch, its cuff links were real. Ditto the suit buttons. As his eyes moved up, he realised he had a real tie on. It was black, and blended into the dark metal, the only thing betraying it was its lack of shine.

Then, finally, he caught the glasses' frame.

They had lenses.

"What the hell is this?" James wondered aloud, staring hard into the statues cold, lifeless eyes.

Which blinked.

Nick had officially made a pre-New Year's Resolution to try and catch his train earlier. So far it had not been going well. He took comfort in it being a *pre*-New Year's Resolution, so come January 1st; it would be officially in practice. This was a warm up.

Actually, this was the first time he had been early. He looked around, surprised. From what he gathered; James never missed this train. He sat on the nearest bench and noticed for the first time that weird statue James mentioned a while ago.

He didn't like it much.

The seven forty-five pulled into Maidenhead and Nick climbed aboard, lingering in the doorway as he waited for his friend. He did not show up and the doors closed.

As the train pulled out, Nick caught a last glance at the statue. It was strange, he thought, the statue didn't match James's description at all. It wasn't elderly. Nor did he wear glasses.

In fact, he thought before immediately shrugging the thought off, it looked like James, more than anyone else.

This world had been killed a thousand times over.

It was something to see.

Vincent Lee sat in the bunker and watched the world burn. The window was of a metre-thick military made transparent material; the light it let through cast a sickly yellow pallor into the room.

In a world dissolving, everything was temporary. And as far as he knew, he was in the last bastion of stability.

"Look at it out there," he muttered, "Just look at it."

"You look at it," came the curt reply behind him. "Same goddamn sight every day. You'd think you'd be bored of it already."

Lee turned and saw his Sergeant, Lou Price, rolling his eyes.

"But it's amazing," he gasped, turning back to the sight. "I had no idea."

"Of course it's amazing," Price said, playing it cool, "It's the end of the bloody world. What did you think it'd look like?"

Lee didn't have an answer. He sat there in awe, and finally mumbled, "I dunno. There's so much. Just… look at it."

"You look at it," Price growled again, feigning annoyance. He was forty-six to Lee's twenty-two, and he got a kick from playing the gruff Sergeant. Lee had just the right mix of naivety and pep to make the dynamic work. Hard to find, especially now.

The boy was right though; it was something to see. From the mountain bunker, they could see for miles, and everything in view was in ruins. Meteors strafed the ground in sharp bursts; the seas boiled and dared to engulf the cities; and the monsters moved throughout, ambling forth like bored titans.

"Morning Vinnie, Lou."

It was Price's turn to look behind him, as a third man emerged behind him, wrapped in a shabby dressing gown.

"Sergeant Price, Keaton," Price warned, bristling. There was nothing about Charlie Keaton he liked. His slumped posture; the inconsistent hours he kept; worst of all, the attitude. "Why aren't you dressed yet?"

"How are the monsters today?" Keaton asked, ignoring the question. The bunker flashed yellow as a ferocious wall of flame struck, illuminating the room but leaving it unscathed. The military knew how to make tough places. Shame they didn't know how to make them comfortable.

Lee jumped back from the fire, mouth wide in amazement. He knew the flame wouldn't penetrate, but some instincts don't go away. Price tightened his grip on his rifle, but didn't react otherwise.

"The big one's cranky today," Keaton said, stifling a yawn.

"Late night, Keaton?" Price asked.

"My body clock's screwed, man. No day; no night. It's just lights on, lights off. You'd think I would have adjusted after a while."

"The soma should have fixed it," Price said. "Have you checked your dosage? It's regulation to do so every two weeks."

Keaton waved a hand, dismissive. Price growled again.

"Sometimes I wonder how they let you in here in the first place," he said.

"Well, for one," Keaton smirked, "I cook the best goddamn risotto you'll ever eat. I guess top brass like it, not that they've ever said. I use extra salt," he added, leaning in for effect. "Figure they don't have to worry about health consequences anymore. That regulation enough for you?"

"Just get to your post," Price hissed. "It's nearly lunchtime."

Keaton yawned again, stretched like a cat, winked at Lee and strolled out.

Price watched him leave and shook his head.

"You don't like him that much, do you?" Lee said.

"He's an utter disgrace."

"I think he's okay," Lee said affably. "Gives this place some character."

"Don't you go listening to a single thing he says," Price warned. "He's a civilian, and a troublesome one."

Keaton returned, now fully dressed, carrying a pot of tea on a tray, half a dozen cups arranged next to it. He approached the dumb waiter next to Price, placed the tray inside and closed it. Pressing a button, the dumb waiter descended.

"What do you think it's like down there?" he asked.

"I'm not paid to ask questions like that," Price said, trying to smother the conversation.

"I reckon it's like the end of Dr. Strangelove," Keaton replied, undeterred. "There's probably a hundred of top brass, with a dozen concubines each, slowly rebuilding the population.”

“Wouldn’t suck,” Lee said, his face lighting up.

“Just doing their bit for the human race,” Keaton grinned. Lee chuckled.

“Don't get distracted,” Price warned them both. “Lee, do your checks.”

“Okay, what’s first?” Lee said to himself, picking up his clipboard. “Ah. Meteorites.”

“Six since last count,” Price reported. “Getting smaller, but should still be considered dangerous.”

“What's a non-dangerous size for a meteorite, Lou?” Keaton teased. “Is there a certain threshold, or can you give it some leeway?”

Lee repressed a grin. Price noticed.

“Don’t you have potatoes to peel, Keaton?”

Keaton shrugged and walked out.

“Next: tectonic movements,” Lee continued. “I got the volcano eruption from last night, plus the tsunami from this morning.”

“There was a tsunami?” Keaton cried, rushing back in. “Holy crap. Did it reach the base?”

“That’s classified,” Price warned.

“Come on,” Keaton moaned. “Who am I going to tell?”

“It reached the base,” Price said, relenting.

“Washed right over us,” Lee added. “Scariest thing I've ever seen. Would give me nightmares for sure if I didn't have the soma.”

“Soma,” Keaton scoffed. “Ha!”

"You know why we take it," Price told him. "It's regulation, to cope with what's going on out there."

"The world's ended. We don't need drugs to deal with that," Keaton said. "That crap turns us into zombies."

"They don't seem to have much effect on you, do they?" Price growled.

"Must be my irrepressible personality," Keaton retorted. "What's your excuse Lou, your mum put it in your bottle, or did you pick up the habit when you signed up?"

Price started. Lee jumped in the way, just in time.

"What's next on the list, Sarg?" he asked Price.

Price's eyes remained fixed on Keaton. "Hostiles," he said.

"Monsters!" Keaton cried, in delight.

Lee shot Keaton a look that read 'I'm trying to help you here!'

Keaton shrugged, grinned, and loped off.

"You shouldn't let him antagonise you," Lee told his sergeant, candidly.

"Why do you care?" Price snapped. "I thought you liked him."

"I do," Lee admitted, "But you're my sarg."

Price couldn't help but smile at that.

"And I don't want to have to keep the peace between you two," Lee concluded. "Just ignore him if you can't get on. Please."

"I'll try. No promises."

They were silent for a moment, then Price spoke. "He is particularly weird today though."

"Yeah," Lee agreed. "Anyway, hostiles."

Price checked to see if they were alone. They were. He grinned, visibly relaxing.

"Okay, there was the two Mothras from this morning, a kraken that washed in from the tsunami, and that momma 'zilla who tried breathing fire on us five minutes ago."

"I'd never have figured you for a Godzilla fan."

"It's why I don't regret signing up. It's really something when they fight, isn't it?"

Keaton re-entered, a tray of appetisers in his arms.

Price instantly regained his stiffness. "... And one second level reptilian biped hostile," he said, resuming the façade of professionalism.

"You and your terminology," Keaton sighed, setting the tray down. "I dunno why you don't call it a Godzilla and be done with it."

He walked out. Lee raised an eyebrow at his sergeant. See? Price considered this as Keaton returned to the dumb waiter with another tray.

"What do you miss about before?" the cook mused.

"We're not supposed to talk about before, remember?" Price reminded him. "Regulations."

"I miss pubs," Keaton said, ignoring him. "Booze. Women. Good times. Can't believe we'll never see that again."

"Keaton!" Price snapped. "We. Don't. Talk. About it."

"Why not?"

"You know why," Price explained. "The soma only deals with so much. It's no good remembering."

"I miss TV," Lee said, suddenly.

"Lee," Price said.

"That's the spirit!" Keaton cheered.

"And football."

"Vince, c'mon..." Price pleaded with the younger man.

"And fooling around with my girlfriend," he added. "It makes you think… all this… it's crazy. It can't be right. Can it?"

"Lee!" Price shouted, shaking Lee's shoulders. "For god's sake, get a grip."

"Sorry," he said, sheepishly, recovering.

"It's okay," Price said. "Double hit the meds tonight. You'll be okay." Turning to Keaton he growled, "As for you…"

"Me?" Keaton said, innocently. "What did I do?"

"What the hell do you think you were doing?" Price shouted. "You know why we don't discuss before! That's why the rules are there: to protect us. Same as the soma."

"Soma," Keaton sniffed with contempt. "Soma's bull, man. Let me tell you something about soma."

He ran into the kitchen, returning with a sock in his hand. It was full of something.

Turning the sock upside down, hundreds of small blue pills spilled out onto the floor to Price and Lee's horror.

"Soma doesn't do jack for anybody," Keaton said, defiantly.

"My god," Lee gasped.

"That's about three months' worth," Keaton said with pride.

"You've got to be kidding me," Price said, disgusted.

"Nope," Keaton grinned. "Now, I've gotta say it's brought on a lot of clarity. See, I've come up with a little theory. Wanna hear it?"

"He's mad," Price warned.

"Hear him out," Lee said, "He's not dangerous."

"Cheers, Vinnie," Keaton said. "Now, I reckon the so-called powers that be, top brass, aren't here. Maybe they're dead; maybe they went off into space, I don't know. But they're not in this bunker."

"See?" Price snorted. "Mad."

"Have you ever spoken to them since you got here?" Keaton asked, "Heard them? Seen them?"

"Well, no, I –"

"Exactly," Keaton smirked

"Keaton, c'mon, they're Top Brass," Lee reasoned. "Just cos they –"

"Now, I've been testing this theory for a while now," Keaton interrupted, "I've been adding spice to their food. A little at first, but recently, it's been a lot. And today's the big test day. The day where the people down there, if they are there, can't ignore us anymore. Wanna see my masterpiece?"

Keaton continued to talk as he walked out. Price and Lee watched him.

"Where's his boot?" Lee asked.

True enough, Keaton was only wearing his left boot. His right foot was exposed, piggies and all.

"How do I know?" Price snapped, "He's lost it. We'll have to subdue him."

Keaton marched back in wearing a proud expression. In his arms was another tray. On the tray was a plate of mashed potato, with, of all things, a black military boot turned upside down in the middle of the mash, poised like a submarine's periscope.

"This regulation enough for you?" he smirked.

"What's going on, Charlie?" Lee asked Keaton.

"If there's anyone down there they'll have to say a few things about this."

"Keaton, you goddamn disgrace!" Price yelled. "Do you think Top Brass are gonna stand for this insubordination? Do you think I will?"

"I think you will," Keaton answered, calmly. "I think if you take your head out of your soma filled arse, you'll want to know. What's so wrong with that?"

Price couldn't believe what he was hearing. He turned to Lee for support.

"Well it's not like we've ever seen Top Brass since we've been here," Lee said, considering the idea. "It wouldn't kill them to come up, at least once."

"Lee, no," Price pleaded, "He's a loon. He's off the soma."

Keaton inserted the boot and mash into the dumb waiter and pressed the button. It descended.

"Wait'll they get the turd crumble for dessert," Keaton smirked.

"This is insane," Price spat.

"It's more insane to believe you've never questioned it," Keaton replied.

Price had started to pace, his world steadily unravelling in front of him.

"I'll prove it to you," he said, trying to convince himself, "You can't insult them like this. They're Top Brass. I'll go and tell them."

"Fine," Keaton told him. "There's no one there though. Let us know how it goes."

"You don't know. You can't prove it."

"Okay then, let's experiment," Keaton said. "You go down. Find Top Brass. I'll go up and leave."

"Leave?" Lee asked.

"Yeah. Monsters? Meteors? Tsunamis? Nah. It's a big joke," Keaton laughed, "We're just rats in a maze. This is the military; they can make us see what they want, especially with the soma. How do we know that's a window and not a TV screen? I'm off."

He went to the main hatch and punched in a code.

Price ran to another door and did the same. He took a last fleeting look at Lee.

"Sarg?" Lee asked.

Price's door opened to blackness and he ran inside, rambling. The darkness consumed him.

"And he called me crazy," Keaton scoffed.

His door opened. Dust was carried in by howling wind, illuminated by a strip of sunlight.

"Coming, Vince?" he asked Lee, a silhouette in the chaos.

"I'm gonna stay put, Charlie," Lee said, unsure of himself.

"Suit yourself," Keaton shrugged, and left through the hatch.

Lee stood in the middle of the bunker, an open door on either side of him, one letting in light, the other leading to shadow. His only company was hundreds of blue pills, scattered all across the floor.

Then a third door opened behind him.

He turned. His reaction was one of stupidity.

"Oh," he said.

Cog

Once there was a city of steel and glass.

In the city, lived a man called Cog. Cog was not a happy man, nor was he unhappy. He was not remarkable, or especially clever. Neither was he handsome, ugly, or unfortunate.

He just was.

Cog's life was not interesting. In fact, it was dull enough that he lived his life in a perpetual daze. When he forgot to pay attention, strange things happened. He would pause for no reason on the threshold when he moved from one room to another; he would walk into walls without either realising it, or feeling pain. And for reasons that totally escaped him, when his toaster released the bread, it did so with a 'pinging' noise he could not explain.

Cog would often dream, but his dreams were as mundane as his life. They gave him a feeling that he had repeated them a thousand times over. Sometimes, but not often, he would do things that did not make any sense; he would run into a lamppost and keep running, not getting anywhere. Sometimes he would dream of falling. These dreams gave him headaches, and he tried not to think about them.

Every day, Cog got up, left his little apartment, and went to work. He took the same route, on the same train with the same faceless commuters, and always arrived at work at the same time.

Cog's job was dull. His office comprised of row upon row of cubicles with 'head top' inhabitants. Although there was no noticeable smell, Cog imagined the air was stale and stagnant. It was so dull that in all honesty he was not sure exactly what he did. He knew no one at work, nor had any desire to. He did not care for his boss. While he did not dislike him, neither was his mind filled with fond memories when he thought of him. Like Cog, he just was.

For this reason, neither Cog, nor his boss had any friends, nor did they seek them out, having never considered having any in the first place.

If he had to name one, Cog's best friend at work would be the man who sat in the booth next to his. He couldn't remember his name, let alone assign it to a face, but once he asked him a question, only to be answered by a pale, bony arm reaching around the divider to point at a sign on Cog's wall that read: *Do not disturb your colleagues. Log a call.*

Cog's routine was rarely interrupted, least of all by himself. A rogue thought of barely noticeable mention concerned a door near his desk. He had never seen anyone use it, and his desire to leave through it was certainly new to him. Trying the handle, he was surprised when the words "The door is locked" materialised in his mind. For a moment he could've sworn they were written in the air in front of him.

One day, on a day like any other, Cog came home from work. He arrived at precisely 5:43, two minutes earlier than usual and therefore a cause for a celebration he would never indulge in, and set about his usual routine. He showered, ate, and watched TV.

Then, for the first time he could remember, something unusual happened.

He saw the glint of a reflection on his television screen. Perhaps human in form, perhaps walking, but certainly – behind him. Cog sank into his chair not knowing what to do; he had no experience of this. He got up, and warily moved towards the kitchen. He peeked round the door, expecting the worst.

In the kitchen, busy rearranging and organising items was another man. He looked just like Cog. He was, in fact, another Cog, for all intents and purposes. Slightly better dressed, a little more composed, but the same man nonetheless. He looked up from his rearranging.

"Hello," said Cog, unsure what the correct protocol was in these situations.

"Hello," replied the other Cog, with a smile.

Cog was quite taken aback, but did not want to seem impolite. "What are you doing?" he asked the other Cog, whom he decided to refer to as Cog 2 for the sake of simplicity.

"I'm moving things," said Cog 2, lifting a microwave from the counter and stacking it near the door.

"Oh," replied Cog, feeling quite unsatisfied with the answer. "Why?"

"Well," said Cog 2, lifting a box and stacking it on top of the microwave, "There's a key on top of that cupboard, and I need to get it."

"Is there?" asked Cog, unaware there ever had been. He had lived in his apartment for as long as he could remember and never knew this. "Why do you need the key?"

"So I can get to Level 2," replied Cog 2, looking a little confused at the question.

Cog shared his confusion, although for a totally different reason. He felt a little unnerved by this other Cog, and wondered whether he should ask him what he was doing in his house. It seemed the thing to do. However, another question came to his lips instead.

"What's Level 2?" he asked, thinking maybe it was a club of some kind, although why he would go to a club was beyond him.

"Level 2's *next*," Cog 2 replied. "It's where I need to go. Don't you need to go there too?"

Cog considered. He didn't know what Level 2 was, but somewhere in the depths of his memory, it seemed to ring a bell. A small bell, muted and rang underwater, but a bell nonetheless.

"You can come with me if you want," offered Cog 2. "They'll just assume you're another player."

Cog thanked him for the offer, but politely declined. Cog 2 frowned slightly, clearly not expecting this answer, but shrugged and smiled once again.

"Are you going to be long?" asked Cog.

"Just 'til I get the key, then I have to find a door for it," replied Cog 2.

Cog pondered, something he seldom did as his routine was always set out for him. He considered asking Cog 2 to leave, but had a feeling he wasn't going to do any harm. In truth, he had always wanted to rearrange the kitchen, watching him do it felt right, but had never got round to it.

Instead, Cog told him it was okay to stay the night if he wanted, and went back to watching TV. He watched his programmes as he always did, but couldn't help but feel troubled. He went to sleep with the sound of Cog 2 moving boxes in the kitchen.

The next morning, Cog went about his regular routine. He showered, shaved (ten perfect strokes with a razor, as usual) and grabbed some breakfast. He approached the kitchen to find Cog 2 making toast, stopping on the threshold as he always did and pausing for a moment. His brow furrowed. He did not like doing that in front of others, not that he knew anyone else. Cog 2 offered him a slice of toast, which he accepted wordlessly.

"That bugs me too," Cog 2 said.

"What's that?" Cog asked, mouth full of toast.

"The loading time between rooms," he answered. "Guess it's one of those things."

"What's a loading time?"

"You know, the time it takes for a room to generate when you enter it. So the frames don't overlap."

Cog stared at him blankly.

"What," Cog 2 scoffed, playfully, "You didn't think it was just you?"

"I dunno," replied Cog, not really sure what was going on. "I thought it was some kinda condition."

"Yeah it's a condition," Cog 2 smiled, "A condition of this world."

"So you have it too?"

"Everyone does," Cog 2 paused, looking concerned. "Well, every character. Your lack of knowledge is quite worrying."

Cog found himself becoming uncomfortable, and changed the subject. "Did you find the key?"

"Bring on Level 2," Cog 2 said, holding up a particularly unremarkable key and grinning. "I'll be looking for the door today."

"Where is it?"

"I dunno. I'll just try doors around 'til it fits. There'll be clues."

"I'm pretty sure you're not allowed to do that," said Cog, warily.

"Nah," said Cog 2, dismissively, "There's no one to bother. No one lives in Level 1." He paused. "Well, except you. Which is weird, to be quite honest."

Cog was, as what was becoming usual for him, quite bemused. This was ridiculous. He had neighbours. This was the city. It's not like every house here was empty. He decided to tell Cog 2 this.

"This is the city, it's not like every house here is empty."

"Actually, it's exactly that," Cog 2 corrected. "Or not even hollow in the first place. Facades, like a movie lot."

Cog pondered. The truth was, he had never been into any other place except work or his home in a long time. He suddenly wondered where he got his food from. It didn't seem too much of a stretch to warrant that this was true.

"Consider this," Cog 2 added, taking the concept one step further, "What if everyone out there, all the other flat, faceless people you've never spoken to and don't seem real to you, are just that. Not real."

Cog didn't know what to say. He expressed this by blinking and looking gormless.

"Come on," said Cog 2, "Involuntary movements you can't control. A perfect routine. Menu screens that appear before your eyes when you select a train ticket? Loading times between rooms?"

The final slice of toast popped out the toaster with its customary cartoon 'ping.'

"That?" he finished, his voice rising a little.

"I'm going to work," Cog said, and went to work.

Cog did as he said. He went to work.

He was cross. Being cross was a strange emotion for him, as he couldn't remember feeling it before. Who was this guy to come and tell him what was what? He didn't even know who Cog 2 was; even his name was made up. That annoyed Cog as well. As it turns out, most things on that journey annoyed Cog.

He was irritated at how the train was exactly on time, which made Cog 2 right. He was vexed at how no other commuters would even look at each other, but would be fully aware of where they were. Again, he saw Cog 2's smug, but admittedly handsome face grinning. He walked into one, who neither flinched, nor reacted, nor apologised, nor got angry. It was as if Cog had simply walked into a wall made of human.

That was it. Cog did something he had never done before: he pushed the man he bumped into, hard.

He was thunderstruck. The poor man had never done anything to deserve being treated like that. Cog had become the epitome of everything he hated. He started to apologise, expecting people to stare and condemn him.

Except they didn't. Even the man he pushed just carried on with his day, completely unawares. Cog followed after him.

"Excuse me," he asked, nervously.

The man said nothing, he didn't even acknowledge he was there.

Cog overtook him, blocking his way. The man stepped round him without seeing him.

"I wanted to apologise for my behaviour…"

The man continued walking. Again Cog ran up to him.

"Lovely weather we're having," the man said, with all the conviction of a telephone queuing system. He walked off.

"Huh," said Cog, to nobody in particular.


Soon after, Cog sat on the train and stared out the window at the streets below. He was afraid to even look at anyone, as he was starting to suspect that they were all living cardboard cut outs.

He watched a man running past others in the street, slam into a lamppost at full speed, then, without apparently feeling a thing, continue to run down the road. He blinked. This was a little odd.

A few minutes later he saw a car drive down the road and stop suddenly. The car appeared to sink a foot or so into the road as if the tarmac was quicksand. The cars behind honked at the inconvenience. Cog didn't know what was weirder; what was happening, the fact that no one seemed to react to it, or that he was only noticing these things now.

Needless to say, Cog's day at work was far from productive. From his booth, he kept staring over at the locked door, until finally he wandered over. No one paid him any attention. They wouldn't, he was only Cog.

Cog tried the door, only this time it was different. He could clearly see the words "The door is locked" written in the air.

He gasped. The other things he had witnessed were weird, but this was amazing! This could very well prove Cog 2 right, and it didn't annoy Cog one bit.

He ran over to his colleague in the booth next to him to show him what he saw. As he started to speak, his colleagues' arm wrapped round the booth and pointed to the sign that read, "Log a call."

"It's nothing to do with work," Cog said, a pleased look plastered over his face.

His colleague didn't reply, just stayed hunched over his desk, his face and body obscured by the cubicle.

"Get up, I want to show you something cool."

His colleague's arm again wrapped round the wall and pointed to the sign, with no more insistence than last time.

"Come on," Cog said, his patience starting to wear thin. He stepped into the booth.

Cog stopped. While he had always been able to see the arm and his back, the rest of the man was just… hollow. He stepped round him to get a better look at his face, and recoiled in horror when he realised he did not have one. There was only a blank space where a face should have been.

Cog 2's words came back to him: that no one else was real, that he was living in a façade. *That no one else was real.* Suddenly, Cog felt very lonely, and very frightened. He had that feeling when you realise you're alone when you thought you had others with you, which was well justified. He ran out the office and headed for the only other person he knew was real.

Cog threw the door to his apartment open with a bang, scaring what can only be described as the crap out of Cog 2. He looked rather distressed, and Cog 2 decided to tell him so.

"You look rather distressed," he said.

"They're not real," gasped Cog, quite clearly out of breath. "None of them!"

"Well that's true, but –"

"No, you don't understand, they're really not real!"

Cog 2 could see how exasperated Cog was, so he humoured him.

"How do you –"

"I punched three businessmen, pushed a pensioner and stole a kids' skateboard!" Cog blurted, "And it doesn't matter, because not one of them was a real person!"

"Well, that's –"

"I uppercutted my boss!" Cog finished.

"Are you quite done?" Cog 2 asked.

Fortunately, Cog was. There were only so many pointless expressions a person could provide at one time to prove the same point, and it turned out five was his limit. They sat in silence for a short while. Finally, Cog spoke.

"Am *I* real?" he asked.

Cog 2 didn't really look sure how to answer, then smiled, and said, "As real as I am."

"And how real is that?"

"I dunno, as real as you I guess."

It was now Cog's turn to smile, although he did not know why. "So, none of this is."

"Pretty much."

"Well, that sucks."

Cog 2 agreed. It did suck.

Cog's smile seemed to sink into his throat as if swallowed by accident. He needed some air. Reeling out of the flat, Cog 2 in tow, Cog tumbled up the stairs to the roof. They stood on the rooftop and watched the fake sun set over the fake city.

Cog looked at the sky. It was a mix of blues, pinks and gold as the sun descended towards the horizon. He saw faults in the sky, as if it was split somehow. The colours rippled and surged unnaturally, as if two images were overlapping and fighting for dominance. "We're not meant to spend too much time here," Cog 2 warned.

Although no tears came, Cog felt like crying. "There's a crack in the sky," he said, his voice hardly a whisper.

"It's out of synch with the refresh rate," Cog 2 explained. "It creates screen tearing."

"It's like the apocalypse."

"Only today," Cog 2 said, reassuringly. "Tomorrow it'll be fine."

"Tomorrow, it'll be as flawed as it always was," Cog managed. "Only they'll have covered it up."

He stepped forwards, closer to the edge. Cog 2 swallowed, looking noticeably more worried. They were at least thirty storeys high.

"Is it just the one life?" Cog asked.

"What?"

"Well, if we're not hollow, and we're meant to do things here, then I'm guessing there are rules to this sort of thing."

"It's in every creature's instincts to preserve its own life," Cog 2 warned.

"Every *living* creature," corrected Cog. "Is that us?"

Cog 2 mulled the question over, then, "I don't know how many and you don't want to test it, but we respawn."

"What's that even mean, respawn?" Cog laughed, a little hysterically. "I'm not a goddamn tadpole!"

"Why don't you come down from there," suggested Cog 2, "And we can go find Level 2."

Cog smiled at his double. Then he stepped onto the edge of the rooftop and jumped off.

*

Cog awoke. Well, awoke was inaccurate. He had not been sleeping. Nor was he lying in his bed, or anywhere else for that matter. He was standing in the middle of his apartment without a scratch on him.

"How was that?" he heard. He turned. Cog 2 was with him.

"That was weird."

"You're telling me. After you jumped I came down here. I figured this is where you would respawn. You just kinda… faded in. Creepy."

Cog shuddered. Although he felt fine physically, he knew, somehow, in the darkest recesses of his mind, that somewhere another Cog was still falling, and would never hit the ground. It was like he had died, and a part of him was not coming back.

"I didn't forget anything," he told Cog 2. "The glitches, the menu screens, the whole lot. I thought I would forget, but I didn't. Is that how you knew? Did you die and remember it too?"

"Yeah," the other man said. "I think we should've played to the end but were forgotten somehow. Maybe this is what happens when people lose interest before they complete it."

Cog nodded, realising something. "Well, there's nothing to stop us from completing it ourselves. It'd be more fun than staying around here."

"That's why I was looking for the key," Cog 2 admitted. "I figure I may as well enjoy my unreality. We just have to find a lock."

"Way ahead of you," grinned Cog, remembering the locked door in his office. "So what's at Level 2?"

"No idea," admitted Cog 2. "Although if you reach Level 7 I've heard you can get a flying car."

"A flying car? What the hell kind of genre is this anyway?"

"I'm going with… neo noir. That's a genre, isn't it?"


Soon after, the two Cogs left the apartment. They reached Cog's work in no time and tried the key. Naturally, it fit, and the door to Level 2 swung open, opening a world of possibility they could not begin to comprehend.

And for all they knew, the world behind them stopped existing the second they stepped through, ready to manifest again when it was needed.

*Pong!*

It was a very odd submarine, thought Ocean, passing through what must have been the vessel's airlock. Yes, his name was Ocean, and he was in a submarine. It wasn't a coincidence.

*Pong.* That sound he knew so well echoed around the room. *Sonar.* *Pong.* It was a cliché of all submarines.

Even alien ones, apparently. This vessel had come up on their own sonar nine hours earlier, and of course Ocean was the one to check it out. At the age of eight, his teacher had suggested to him that with a name like that, a career in the navy was the way forward. War had yet to reach Adonis back then, but fourteen years later, when it did, Ocean was enlisted and prepared to do his duty.

He even sent the teacher, Mr Loddon, a card thanking him when he made it into the Special Ops team. Mr Loddon never wrote back.

*Pong.*

"They have sonar too," said Jenkins, behind him, "What're the odds?"

Ocean didn't really get Jenkins – he had a thing for alien cultures and seemed to find everything about the world of Adonis fascinating – whereas Ocean was just there to do a job.

"But the sub's abandoned," Ocean observed, "Why's it still running?"

"We don't *know* it's abandoned," Jenkins said. "We detected a life form of some kind, it just didn't correspond to any of *them*."

By *them*, Jenkins meant their adversary in the war. Like the humans, their opponents – nicknamed 'crabs' because their name in their native tongue was unpronounceable without mandibles – were not native to Adonis. Both species were squabbling over Adonis's natural resources, which were ample. The conflict was fierce. The crabs were named accordingly because of their crustacean-like appearance, and used bio-tech weapons, something Ocean felt was a perversion of science.

Of the natives of Adonis, there was no sign. There were rumours, of course. Some intelligence reports claimed they had been coerced into working for the crabs and couldn't be trusted. Others said they were mindless brutes who refused to join either side. A third report, which Jenkins had taken a shine to, claimed that they were an enlightened race, pacifists, and had retreated to the vast and labyrinthine network of underwater caverns that made up the core of Adonis.

*Pong.*

Ocean decided not to retort; Jenkins's semantic observations were not worth taking the time to argue over, and wordlessly they set about exploring this mysterious and alien submarine.

*Pong.*

Ocean made sure the camera on his helmet was recording as they made their way through the alien vessel. It was unlike anything seen by mankind before; the whole sub was made up of organic matter, with walkways, tunnels and platforms made up or rigid carapaces, cartilage and bone. The air was breathable, and the temperature regulated. It was very impressive.

"Maybe the crabs were on to a good thing," Jenkins mused to Ocean's reluctant (and silent) agreement.

*Pong.*

They searched together high and low, supposing the purpose of each room or chamber as they found them. They knew the bridge was what they needed to find, and they proceeded in the direction they assumed it was in. Whether they were right or not was anyone's guess.

"So, we're just speculating where the bridge is then?" Jenkins shrugged.

"We're moving in a calculated and coordinated sweep," Ocean told him, then, half smiling as he recognised the lack of both calculation and coordination added, "But yeah, that's about right."

"Ocean, was that a joke?" Jenkins gasped, a huge and infectious smile spreading across his face.

*Pong.*

"Don't tell anyone," Ocean warned him. "I just wish I knew where that bloody sonar was coming from."

"You and me both," Jenkins agreed as they made their way into another room. As with every other one this room was also deserted, but they kept their guard up. *Something* was alive on the sub, and they were determined to find it.

"Wherever the bridge is, it's not up here," Ocean concluded. "Let's stay at the front but see if we can move down to the base. You never know."

"Roger that."

The marines did just that. They had entered the sub at the back of the vessel and moved forwards, effectively covering most of the top half. So far, nothing.

But the bottom half remained uncharted, and full of potential.

A route downwards presented itself; two holes in the floor – vertical tunnels, it turned out, only slightly wider than they were – which they slowly descended. The route was tricky, and like cavers they had to wedge their backs to the wall and press their arms and knees to the opposite side. Ocean felt a current of air shooting up and around him. *Pong*. And that bloody sonar! If anything it seemed to be getting louder.

Eventually the tunnels ended; they realised this when their feet had nothing else to purchase, and the way opened out into a large chamber, ten feet below them. The marines dropped, landing expertly, ready for anything.

*Pong*.

No crabs met them. They had not burst into the alien stronghold. This room, like every other, was deserted. The chamber was the largest room they had yet to explore, and one of the most unusual. Its floor was a huge, leathery material; three of the curved walls were enamelled with what looked like giant piano keys; and the ceiling was arched majestically. The same air current they felt coming down the tunnels moved all around them. For the first time, Ocean noticed the air pulsed in bursts, and on every other pulse, the *pong* of sonar was audible.

"Okay…" Ocean murmured, feeling incredibly unsettled.

*Pong.*

He and Jenkins exchanged nervous glances.

*Pong.*

Ocean looked at the fourth wall in the chamber; the only one without the giant piano keys on them. In its centre was a huge, sealed iris that they guessed could be a sealed airlock.

But to where?

It couldn't be the one they had entered the sub in, which had been in the far end; the arsehole, as Jenkins had dubbed it on approach. This must be it, they realised, the core; the sub's centre. Where answers lay.

*Pong.*

And, as ever, the sonar continued to ping, endlessly, like a pulse or metronome.

"Any ideas how we get in there?" Jenkins asked.

Ocean shook his head, the alien bio-tech completely beyond him.

"It could be anything," he mused, pushing around the organic matter of the back wall for a hidden panel. Jenkins joined in, and for the next few minutes they poked and prodded the wall, the giant piano key things, and the odd bumps and nobbles on the leathery floor. Nothing.

"It's like the sound effect of a sonar," Jenkins said, growing annoyed by its consistency, "Y'know, like in old movies when they want to show that characters are in a submarine. White enclosed rooms, periscopes and that sound." He did an impression of the sound, stretching out the vowel. *"Pong. Pong."*

*Pong.*

"Yeah," Ocean agreed, remembering playing war at school. Once Ocean had got the idea of joining the navy in his head that was all he wanted to play. It was little wonder he didn't have a lot of friends growing up.

Unbeknownst to either marine, the floor had shifted slightly underneath them; the leathery material almost gathering itself up, tilting them at a slight angle.

"I could never get the sound right though," Ocean remembered, trying the 'pong' noise himself.

"That sounds more like…" Jenkins trailed off. His eyes widened.

"Breathing," Ocean finished. His eyes darted round the chamber and he realised what the room reminded him of: the inside of a mouth.

That was when the iris on the fourth wall opened, revealing nothing but blackness.

In the same movement, the floor threw them towards it in an almighty heave, like a Mexican wave of fleshy material.


Ocean and Jenkins were not seen again, but the footage they recorded was received by one of their own side's reconnaissance vessels hours later. Upon reviewing it, the analysts were reported to have summarised the following:

"Without the advantage of perspective, Jenkins and Ocean were ignorant to what was apparently in front of them the entire time. This startling lack of judgement, when taken in context, makes for an event that our navy would best forget, especially when summarised concisely."

They had a point. And so it was that the Adonian Sub-Whale was discovered. A (mostly) harmless creature, the navy declined to name the creature after either marine, given that in summary, all they achieved was climbing into the creature via its rectum and somehow escaping entering its stomach through means of a lucky break, only to willingly enter its mouth and be consumed.

Pong.

# A Biting Lie

When I was nine or ten (or possibly eleven, but I hope not), I bit another kid at school. It's a weird thing to remember, because the whole thing is so unlike me it's hard to believe I did it.

I think that's how I got away with it. No one was better behaved than me; my behaviour was *flawless*. I mean, it had to be, for reasons I'll mention later. I don't say this with pride – the opposite, actually – just objectivity. I was a well-behaved kid.

So why bite? I don't remember really. I think it's because this kid was just acting like such a dick.

It was one of those lunchtimes where my friends weren't around. Either they were playing football and I didn't want to, or it was one of those days where something was going around and kids were dropping like flies. I'm one of the lucky ones, I don't tend to get ill.

Regardless, me, the boy-about-to-be-bitten and another few kids, were hanging out. I don't really remember who he was now, but I'm pretty sure I hadn't hung out with him before, he probably was in the year below me. (I certainly wouldn't hang out with him again.) This boy was sat on the top of this picnic bench, whereas I was sat on the seat. You know, where you're supposed to sit.

He was doing that thing which all bullies do, which is make themselves look better by making other kids look bad. I thought, and still think, this is childish, cowardly and crappy.

Whatever, we were kids. Maybe I shouldn't have been so principled about it.

Cut to: me biting him. I don't remember the final straw, it was probably something tiny, and as he was sat on the picnic bench's top, I had a clean run at his leg.

*Chomp.*

Just a nip. Didn't even break the skin. But the noise he made; you'd have thought I'd have ripped flesh from bone.

A wail to a less than sympathetic dinner lady (was there any other kind?) and I found myself outside the headteacher's office, waiting. It was weird; I'd never been in this position: the primary school equivalent of awaiting sentencing.

I should have been terrified – more so than perfectly behaved, I was also an exceptionally anxious child, I once cried when I forgot my pencil case – and this was the worst place a child could be at Oaklands Junior School. But instead I was utterly detached. Fascinated, even.

I was shown into Mrs. Baughan's office, where she regarded me with suspicion, concern, and a smattering of surprise. I never had any problem with her – rarely saw her, aside from assemblies – but she knew who I was. Hence why she seemed so surprised to see me there.

This was a mistake, surely.

Well, my behaviour over the years at Oaklands had built up some credit, so rather than yelling at me, or worse, putting me in *The Green Book*, the greatest punishment known to Oaklands, she asked me what happened.

In retrospect, I'm not sure how I managed this. I've never been this inventive in my life. But, as ever, the answer came from comic books.

Around this time, I was an avid reader of *Transformers* comics, and British reprints – printed on A4, naturally – had back up strips. *Transformers* had *Action Force*, which became *GI Joe*, but they were the same thing. In one issue, a young thief steals a bag from an old blind man, who deftly throws his cane between the boy's legs, tripping him up. The police arrive to arrest the boy, and the blind man – who's totally a ninja – says *he* tripped, the boy went to help him, tripping on the cane. The police somehow buy this (there's some head scratching, some "I coulda sworn I saw it different,") leave the boy be, and – bam! – the ninja has a new apprentice.

So basically, I tried that. I tripped, fell into the bench, and my teeth dug into the boy's leg. If he hadn't been sitting on the bench's table top, he wouldn't have been bitten.

I don't know what was worse, the bite, or that I'd looked into my headteacher's eyes and lied.

And Mrs. Baughan bought it. I left without punishment. I don't remember ever seeing the boy again, but whatever, he was a dick. He got sick afterwards, but that was inevitable, I suppose. Not that anyone linked his illness with the bite.

They rarely do.

I'm discreet like that, what with my good behaviour and all.

Never in school. That was my rule. It's why I was amazed I'd broken it this time.

Still, it was probably for the best he got sick. If he didn't get sick then he would've turned, and that would've been worse. I can't stand it when they turn.

Most others that turn can't handle the sunlight. That would've attracted too much attention. I'm not saying he would have necessarily burst into flames on the playground, but it's not too far from that. I'm lucky: the sunlight doesn't harm me. I don't know why that is, but I'm not complaining.

I hadn't thought about this in years, don't know why it's come to me now. But one thing that comes to mind when I reflect over the only time I let my true nature get the better of me at school is this:

Teachers aren't idiots. My story was clearly crap, and I'd thought at first that Mrs. Baughan had let me get away with it because of my good behaviour to date, but she knew what I was.

Sitting in class, anxious all the time, I must have seemed like a time bomb.

She must have been terrified that this one act could open the floodgates, that I'd be devouring my way through the school in no time. I could've. Some days, I was sorely tempted.

There's only one thing I can conclude from this: she must have weighed up who I'd bitten and thought, "meh, let him."

*That's* how much of a dick this kid was.

"Can I go on your phone?" asked Paige, six and a half.

"No," her mum told her, again.

"I want to go home," she said.

"We've been over this," her mum said, again, not for the first time. "You've got to see the dentist."

There was literally nothing interesting about the dentist's waiting room. Nor was there anything to do there. Paige articulated her boredom the way she knew how.

"Uhhhhhhn," she moaned through gritted teeth.

"Stop that," her mum managed to say without snapping. "You just have to be patient. It'll be your turn soon, and you're going in, whether you want to or not."

Paige got up, went to the table of magazines for what must have been the fifth time, found there was still nothing there worth reading, and sat down.

"Please can I go on your phone?"

"No. I've got bits to sort out." It was mostly true, although the main reason her mum didn't hand it over was because then she'd have nothing to do herself.

Paige's legs swung under the plastic chair. Every now and then her feet would swing back far enough that she was able to bump her heels on the underside of the seat with a satisfying thump.

As her mum opened her mouth to tell her to stop doing this, Paige said, "Ellie Saunders says the dentist is where they take all your dreams away and make you a growed up."

"Well, obviously Ellie Saunders hasn't been to the dentist often," her mum said. She thought Ellie's parents rarely went to the dentists by the look of them, and decided it would be best not to share her opinion on this with her daughter.

"She has. She says the dentist is an anack… and anorak… an ah…"

"A what?"

"You know. One of those that stands for stuff. Like PC, or TV or, what's the one Uncle Scott says which you won't tell me what it means? MILF?"

"Okay!" her mum hissed, suddenly painfully aware that there were a few people sat nearby. No one seemed to have heard them. "An acronym."

"Yeah!" Paige agreed. "An acronym. She says it's… um… Dreams End with New Teeth."

"That's not a very good acronym," her mum said. "There's no 'W' in dentist. And she left off the 'ist'."

"It's a little 'W'," Paige shrugged, as if this was a non-issue, "and it's probably just 'D.E.N.T.' anyway. 'Ist' is what they do. So I don't think I'll be going in there. I don't want to be a growed up."

"It's grown. *Grown* up. Anyway, the dentist here is nice. You've never had a problem with Dr. Singh, have you?"

Paige stared at her feet, as if now she didn't have anything to say.

"Have you?" her mum repeated.

"No," Paige said moodily.

"Well there you go."

"But he never took away my teeth before," Paige said in a sudden burst of passion. She slumped down into the plastic chair and muttered. "I don't *want* to be a growed up."

Her mum sighed. She realised this wasn't going to go away any time soon and put her phone in her handbag.

"Why does having some teeth removed make you a grown up then?" she asked. "I suppose I should know if you're going to make such a fuss about it."

"'Cos it happens to everyone. You lose your baby teeth and you moan and you become a growed up and you stop having fun."

"Well, I don't have any baby teeth, and I still have fun. Don't you think I'm fun?"

Paige shot her mother one of those black looks that kids can somehow get away with.

"Andy and I used to have fun. Then they took his teeth away and now all he does is watches football and talks about girls."

"It didn't happen that fast," her mum told her. "At least, I hope it didn't. Andy's just growing up a bit. He still loves playing with you though."

"Don't matter," Paige mumbled. "I won't want to play with anyone when they take away my teeth."

"You'd look weird with those baby teeth in a grownup head," her mum teased. "Anyway, no one's taking them away, they just fall out of their own accord. Although Dr. Singh did say you'll probably have an overcrowded mouth and some of them might need to be removed when they come in.”

Mother and daughter exchanged looks. At that moment, Mum realised her mistake.

Whaaaaat?” Paige gasped. “He’s going to take them out *after* new ones have grown? That’s even worse!”

“Just so they grow straight and properly!” her mum explained, placatingly. She realised she was suddenly on the back foot and paused, regaining her composure. “Look. Don’t you want good teeth?”

“I don’t want new teeth. I want *my* teeth.”

“New teeth will be better for you though. They’re bigger and stronger and won’t fall out. Why don’t you want new ones?

“*Because*,” Paige sighed, as if they’d been through this too many times and she couldn’t believe she was having to explain this yet again. “Dreams. End. With. New. Teeth. I want to keep my dreams. That means I have to keep my teeth.”

“Why do dreams end with new teeth? Grownups dream too. I dream all the time. Sometimes, I dream even when I’m at work.”

“Yeah, but they’re not real dreams. They’re not real like mine are.”

“I dunno. I think they’re all right.”

“Really,” Paige said. She knelt on her seat to give her mum her full attention. Her mum felt like she was suddenly on the receiving end of an interrogation. “What did you last dream about then?”

“Well. I dreamt that you, me, Andy and Daddy all went to the seaside.”

"Yeah? What did we do there?"

"You all had lots of fun."

"And what did you do?"

"I… I had to do work when I sat on the beach."

"See!" Paige practically exploded. "That's rubbish! That's not a real dream at all!"

"I dreamt more than that," her mum added.

"Oh yeah?" Paige added with a touch too much sarcasm for her mother's tastes. "What other exciting stuff did you dream then?"

"Well, I was at work, but the building looked totally different."

"Different… how?" Paige asked with narrowed eyes.

"It didn't have a ceiling. You could see the sky."

"Okay," Paige nodded.

Her mum didn't say anything but looked proud of herself.

"Oh!" Paige said. "You're done."

"Fine then, what did you dream last night?" her mum asked, feeling a bit crestfallen. At least she remembered her dreams. She often didn't.

"Well," said Paige, "I dreamed I rode my bike to the moon but when I got there it was made out of this sponge like in those squishy foam pits at the trampoline park but you could eat it and then I flew around through big caves that looked like the inside of a washing machine…"

"Okay, that's pretty impressive, but –"

"And then I went in a whirlpool and came out into some place that looked like Grandma's house but the piranhas let me out so I left…"

Paige continued, her mum realising she had only paused for breath. She continued for a while longer until she trailed off.

"Are you done now?" her mum asked.

"There was more but I can't remember it," Paige announced.

"I hope you use these dreams at school," her mum told her. "They probably make for good paintings for Miss Ridley."

"Don't you wish you dreamed stuff like that? Your dreams are boring."

"Yeah, but I think they'd tire me out. I just want to relax when I'm asleep."

"Nanny says when you were little you used to dream like me. In your dreams you had a friend who looked like the Michelin Man."

"I did," her mum said, the response slipping out almost involuntarily as she remembered. "He was called Clive."

"What's a Michelin Man, Mummy?"

"He was like a cartoon character for a place that sold –"

"When did you stop dreaming like me?" Paige interrupted, deciding this new question was the more important one and couldn't wait.

"I think I must have been around your... oh."

The door to the dentist's room opened and Dr Singh, the kindly family dentist stepped out.

"Weren't you happier then?" Paige asked her mother.

"Ready, Paige?" Dr Singh asked.

As Paige and her mum stood up, Mum's phone buzzed. She took it out of her handbag.

"It's work," she said. "I'm sorry, I need to take this."

"That's all right," Dr Singh said. "We should be all right together, what do you think Paige? We'll just have a look around, see what's going on."

"Okay," Paige beamed. She did actually quite like Dr Singh, and her previous reluctance was now apparently forgotten.

"Oh. Okay," her mum said. "If you're sure…"

Mum answered her phone. She barely heard the voice on the other end of the line as her daughter and the dentist disappeared into the small room, the red door closing behind them as Paige climbed into the chair.

"What's that?" Paige's mum asked the caller when they repeated a question. "I'm sorry, I was in a world of my own."

She returned to her seat and tried her best to focus on the call, but try as she might, her eyes kept straying to the red door.

The Boastful Turtle

Folklore and fairy tales are not always kind stories, but we view them through a small window where nothing can get in or out. Mistakes are made and lessons learned. There is a moral to be gleamed from what you're told. With fairy tales, as with real life, whether a story is kind or not depends on when you choose to stop reading.

It is most definitely worth bearing that in mind here…

Some animals are more fortunate than others. The Tamaraw buffalo are strong, the Calamian deer have antlers to fight off predators, and the crocodiles of the Agusan marsh are stealthy. But many would say that birds are the most fortunate creatures of all. Turtle certainly thought so. He was unlike the others. Where most turtles were grateful that their flippers meant they could swim in the sea, this turtle moaned that they were not wings. Where most turtles knew that their hard shells would protect them from predators, this turtle felt only a weight on his back that meant he would never be light enough to take to the skies. Flying was all he talked about, and he bored the other animals to tears by talking about it all of the time. When he wasn't talking about flying, he was talking about himself. This particular turtle was not exactly good company.

"You should be happy with what you've got," one of the elders told him after he had been on an especially long rant about flying. This elder was a wise and ancient beast with as many scars on his shell as lines on his face. The young turtles claimed the elder had once met Bathala, the caretaker of the earth. This had happened many, many years ago when Bathala had first created life. The wise elder would neither confirm nor deny this rumour, but Turtle did not care. All he cared about was flying.

Turtle's obsession meant that he had few friends. He did not much care for the other turtles who just wanted to swim and eat. And he resented all of the birds because they could fly and he could not. But he knew that if he ever was going to fly, he would need a bird to help him. It was that or ask one of the Monsters of the Philippines, and he was smart enough to know not to interfere with them. The only creatures stupid enough to ask favours of the Aswangs and the Wakwaks were the humans, and those who asked were never seen again.

Instead, Turtle decided to ask a goose. This was long ago you understand, back in the days when animals asked each other questions. He knew that geese were very fussy birds. But they were also not particularly bright, and so Turtle thought that he would have no problem getting them to help.

The goose that Turtle chose to approach was, at the time, off to meet her flock and did not relish the thought of trying to teach a turtle how to fly - especially *this* turtle.

It seemed like an awful lot of work.

"My flock is migrating for the cold season and I am very busy," the goose told Turtle. This was partly true, but the goose also hoped to avoid hurting his feelings. After all, everybody knew that turtles could not fly no matter how determined they were.

"I really don't care about how busy you are," whined Turtle, selfishly. "I want to fly and I want to fly now!"

It was obvious to the goose that the insistent turtle would not take no for an answer.

"Let me first ask my flock," she said, knowing full well what they would say. She could have flown off then and there, but she had either a big heart or a small brain.

The response she got from her flock was just what she expected, and the air filled with loud, derisive honks as the geese all laughed at Turtle's ridiculous demand. Once the laughter had subsided, one goose who was more thoughtful than the others voiced an unconventional idea.

"If two of us held a strong stick between us," he said, "then Turtle could hold on while we flew. He does have a strong beak and could surely hold the stick while in flight. He would have to be very careful," he added. "If he let go, even for a second, he would fall and he would be too heavy for us to catch."

The goose didn't fancy this idea very much and hoped that the thought of falling to the ground would be enough to put Turtle off the plan altogether. But, being a very selfish and single minded sort of creature, Turtle was determined to go ahead.

"Well, just remember to hold on as tightly as you can and never let go," said the goose, "Otherwise you will fall and we will not be able to save you. You look very heavy with that shell of yours."

"Yes, yes, of course," said Turtle, utterly distracted by his own excitement. He was too busy picturing himself flying with the geese to pay heed to any warnings. He was also busy thinking how jealous his friends would be when they saw him flying high up in the sky above their heads.

And so, with Turtle's jaw clenched firmly down on the stick held between them, the two geese took off with a whooshing sound and a flapping of their powerful wings. Having never flown before, Turtle was amazed at the myriad of sights that stretched out below him as the geese soared up into the clear blue skies: the beautiful canopy of the jungle, the winding rivers; everything he saw only served to prove to Turtle that he had witnessed far too little of the world.

But rather than being humbled by the amazing sights all around him, rather than simply enjoy the experience, selfish Turtle wanted to shout out to the animals below. He wanted to brag and boast about what he could see. And he especially wanted to shout down to all of those turtles who told him that he would never fly.

And that was when he opened his mouth.

Remember how I said that folklore and fairy tales are not always kind stories? Well now you see why. Our story ends with Turtle falling. But we never see him land. Does he hit the ground? He should. That is how these things work. And if he does… well there is the moral to our story. Can you guess what that moral might be?

But this is folklore and fairy tale – a strange place where anything is possible, where there are talking animals who do things they know they should not do.

So, for the benefit of this story, maybe he never lands. And in that respect, if Turtle falls for an eternity, doesn't that mean he's flying after all..?

It was the day after I came home with a bloody nose that Papi first took me to the allotment. I didn't want to call my granddad Papi – the name was stupid – but Mum and Dad weren't around anymore, and it was his rules. I was too young to argue. I got the message: we're in France, and you've got to respect that, it doesn't matter where you're from. Maybe that was why I got in the fight. I was a British in a French school and proud of it. It wouldn't have gone well the other way round, what did I expect?

"No perspective," was all Papi could say, with no further explanation.

We walked to the allotment in silence. It was early morning and the sun was climbing skyward, starting to bear down on us already. The only sounds were the fleeting breeze ruffling the trees that brought the only respite from the heat, and the endless buzzing of cicadas which reminded me how still it was. Papi's English was as bad as my French, so our conversations were brief at best; mumblings in broken and simple phrases, the language divide bridged by ineffective gesturing.

That day, like every time that followed, he made me carry a large wicker basket I struggled to see over. In it was a pair of shears, a long coil of rope, a trowel, our lunch, and an empty coffee jar. Papi carried nothing. He had flown planes for the Free French over North Africa in the War, or so I had been told, until a bullet had taken a chunk out of his leg. I didn't know why a pilot even needed good legs to fly, but the barrier between us meant I couldn't ask him even if I wanted to. I couldn't imagine Papi as a pilot. I couldn't imagine him as anything other than an old man.

The allotment seemed limitless – square plot after plot adorned with the fruits of people's efforts: mouth-watering raspberries and tomatoes, plump courgettes and vines of haricot vert, and vivid flowers of every colour and shade. Sunflowers smiled at me as we passed them.

When Papi showed me his plot, my heart dropped. Unlike the others I had seen which were drenched in colour and loaded with fruit, this was an unloved, dry square of dirt in the corner, riddled with weeds and stewarded by dozens of slugs.

"Back again, Edouard?" an old man asked Papi. His name was Jean-Paul, I found out later. He was much fatter than Papi and owned the three allotments next to ours. He casually plucked a ripe tomato from one of his vines with his plump fingers and inspected it with glee, before adding it to the pile of vegetables he had collected. "What is it this time," he teased, "Another money tree? You should try and grow easier crops. You know you can't grow anything in that dirt!"

"So what?" Papi replied, although he did not seem to mind much.

"Easier crops, more produce," Jean-Paul chuckled, and left us to it. I looked from his allotment to ours in despair. He might have had a point.

"No perspective," Papi said, then, to me, "Your problem, too."

I frowned. I didn't know what he meant. I could see things just fine.

Papi took the empty coffee jar from the basket. He stooped awkwardly, picked up a slug from the ground and put it in the jar. He handed the jar to me and gestured for me to do the same. Lovely.

I did as he instructed and picked up a slug. It was fat and slimy and did not like being held one bit. I quickly put it in the jar. "Continue," said Papi.

I carried on, while my grandfather got to his knees awkwardly and slowly turned the soil with his trowel. The slugs I was catching moved faster than he did.

"What are we doing, Papi?" I asked after a while, frustrated with how slowly he was working, "What are you growing?"

"So what," Papi said, to my frustration. Maybe he wasn't listening.

The days continued like this for a while, and I hated them at first. Early in the morning and late afternoon we turned the soil and collected slugs. Almost every day we went, before and after school for me, and every weekend. We avoided going at midday, because no self-respecting Frenchman would go then, I gathered. There was no point, working in such heat for no reason.

Every day was the same thing, soil and slugs, slugs and soil. Carrying the basket, making sure we had the same gear. At home, testing and strengthening the length of rope, mending the basket, reinforcing it. Over and over and over and over.

And it was there that, while everything stayed the same, everything changed. I didn't know what it was about the allotment, but knowing I was going there, and knowing on the way back that I would be going again tomorrow, it made me feel calmer somehow. I still didn't like school: I missed my friends and didn't care much for the French kids, but I didn't mind them much either. One day the one who gave me a bloody nose tried to start on me, but I let it slide. "So what," I said.

One day we saw Jean-Paul again, smugly collecting his produce. He howled in disbelief as Papi sprinkled salt into the dirt of our allotment, calling him a crazy old fool.

I hadn't notice Papi doing this before; I had been too busy collecting slugs. "Papi, if we salt the earth, nothing will grow on it," I told him.

"So what?" Papi shrugged.

"The boy's right!" Jean-Paul agreed, "Nothing grows on salted earth."

He walked off, laughing to himself, and repeating the words "Crazy old fool," again and again.

"Papi," I asked, "Why are we doing this if we can't grow fruit or vegetables?"

"Not growing fruit and vegetables," he said, with a mischievous twinkle in his eye, "So what."

And that was that. I couldn't argue with him if I couldn't understand him.

Then, a few days later, the storm came. It snuck in early before I awoke, but quickly made its presence known. Shutters banged and the dogs hid. Lightning lit up the sky.

"Pierre!" Papi beamed, bursting into my room as I sat up. "Pierre!" I had never seen him so excited about anything.

"Papi?" I murmured, only half awake and rubbing the sleep from my eyes.

"Allotment!" he cried, "Vite!"

We almost ran there, in the wind and the rain, yet Papi moved faster than I had ever seen before. His leg hardly seemed to bother him, and he was almost skipping. As ever, I struggled under the cumbersome basket and its contents. Papi made sure I remembered them. The storm was laying waste to the allotments. Jean-Paul would be furious. Bean plants clung to the canes they snaked around like sailors to a sinking ship, but it didn't stop them being flattened. It was clear that wasn't what Papi wanted to show me.

It was our patch.

"What… is that?" I asked, dumbfounded, while the winds whipped at my face.

"That *is* What," Papi replied, taking the basket out of my arms as I stared ahead, slack jawed. "So what," he explained, "*Sow*. We sowed this."

The best way to describe "What" was to think of an explosion going off in a paint factory over a cluster of impossible shapes. The plant was, without a doubt, the most beautiful and extraordinary thing I had ever seen, even in the wind and rain.

Overnight, or maybe it was just now, the plant had risen from the arid soil Papi had turned and salted daily, and exploded into bloom. It was maybe eight foot high, with a smooth green trunk and leaves like giant sycamore seeds or enormous feathers, in every colour known to man and maybe a few previously unseen. At the base of the leaves, close to the stem, hung football sized pods that bounced and jangled soundlessly.

In the wind it looked so *alive*, stretching and twisting away from the earth towards the sky.

That's when I realised it actually *was* trying to escape the earth, the leaves catching the strong currents and the pods tugging at the roots that grounded it. The pods were weightless, it seemed, like tiny balloons and was trying to pull the plant up.

As I gawped, Papi got to work. It took me a few moments to realise what he was doing. He tied two lengths of the rope to either side of our basket, and looped it round the body of the What, fastening it in an intricate knot. He then stepped into the basket, testing its weight.

"In," he smiled, pointing at the basket.

I did as he ordered, feeling ridiculous as we huddled together in the wicker carrier.

Once we were in, Papi got the shears from the basket and cut away at the stem.

"Papi, you can't kill it," I protested, "It's just grown."

"Flower and seeds," he explained, "The rest is below, will grow again."

Fair enough, I thought.

"Hold tight," he said, and with three sharp hacks, snipped the shears through the stem.

Without the stem to anchor it, the What slowly lifted into the air, catching the wind. It was followed by the ropes, which eventually tightened. When the ropes could stretch no further, the basket was gently pulled from the ground, with us in it.

The basket lurched to and fro as it was tossed about by the winds, and we swung into the shed in Jean-Paul's allotment with a terrific thud. The shed was a rickety, rotten old frame of wood, but it managed to keep itself together. When we hit it a second time, it collapsed pathetically. Even over the winds, I heard Papi chuckle, before a strong gust caught us and sent us higher into the air.

I remember holding on very tightly to Papi then, and I must have closed my eyes.

As we lifted, I felt the summer sun warm my face as the rains subsided and the clouds parted: the storm was over as soon as it had begun, yet the winds continued to howl, and the basket lurched and swung under the What.

"Pierre," said Papi, "Open your eyes."

I did as he said, and looked.

We were very high up. Underneath us stretched the French countryside. For mile after mile were fields, meadows, and woods, a tapestry of greens and browns. There were rivers too, glittering in the sunshine. From this height, it looked like a map, and I could pick out train lines, roads, bridges, churches and houses; all the signs of man's efforts to try and control their world.

"When I flew, things made sense," Papi explained kindly, "Important you see it too. Distance from your problems gives perspective."

It was then that I saw. The kids at school; not fitting in; being away from my friends, at the end of the day, none of it really mattered when you looked at the big picture. Because any problem can be overcome given enough time, and the help of those who love you. And here, I had both.

Far below us, with the rains ended, some of the children from school emerged from their homes to play. Those who noticed the What stared up in disbelief.

I would be fine. He knew I understood, but I told him so anyway.

"And if not, we have these," he grinned, opening the coffee jar of slugs and holding one between thumb and forefinger. "Like in the war. Bombs away!"

"Thanks Papi," I said, before adding nervously, "How do we get down?"

"Later," Papi chuckled, "When we are ready. We can stay up here a while. So what if we drift a ways, we can always find our way back."

I smiled. So what indeed?

The Dream Job

While every person on the planet is different from one another, few people are like Arthur Sleep. Arthur was different, because in dreams he was awake, whereas you and I are not.

Arthur did his most important work while his body slept. That's where his job was, in dreams. Arthur was a temp, which was sensible because dreams are not permanent, after all. His job would change from night to night. Some would be spent teaching the parroting giraffes more words, which was important, because they mostly just said 'what?' which was a bit annoying.

Other nights, Arthur was a handyman. He would tend to rainbows if they needed a lick of paint. He made sure to add the extra colours they lacked in the waking world, the ones that are remembered as soon as they are seen, but do not make it through to the day. You might not know what I'm talking about, but you're awake while you read this. If you were reading this while asleep, you'd understand. But then, you can't do that, because you're not Arthur Sleep.

Arthur's waking world might have been our sleeping one, but his sleeping world was our waking one. He saw our waking world through the veil of a dream. This caused some bother. Because of this, people did not understand him, and he did not understand them.

Time made little sense to Arthur. He did not understand having to pay money when the numbers said one thing, or needing to arrive when others said something else. He said things that didn't always come out right because he was asleep, and you don't say things that make sense when you're asleep.

In the waking world, he did not fit in.

When Arthur was truly awake – in the world of dreams – he was terribly punctual. He knew when he had to plant the rows of glowing solar frogs that provided mobile runway lights for night flights, or when to trim the Never-When, which got thick and matted with time if not properly and regularly tended to. He could manage a hundred different things with ease. It all made sense, and he was happy.

Arthur's job, or the job people in the waking world believed he had, was a gardener. It was a small garden in the grounds of a ruined castle, in the heart of a busy town, and he tended to them with care, albeit in his own unusual manner, and in his own time. He could have been fired from the grounds over his eccentricities, but the council that ran it were quite relaxed, paid him little, and worried they would face a lawsuit if they dismissed someone so… unusual.

The garden was maybe the only quiet place in the town, and businessmen would come there at lunch to find a little peace and a place to think while they ate their sandwiches and pre-packed salads.

It was on a day like this, a day like any other, that a new businessman came to the gardens, one Arthur had not seen before, although they did all look alike to him. Apparently he had a very important job, that involved a lot of meetings – and meetings about meetings – and he rarely took lunch, but he had recently been told he needed to take some time for himself every day for the sake of his health.

Simply put, his heart worked, but if he kept on going the way he had been, it would explode and wouldn't work anymore. That would be bad.

The Businessman was miserable, Arthur could tell. He didn't stop to think why in any way that would make sense to you or me. He couldn't tell if he was unhappy because due to his enforced breaks he had less time to send emails, not being allowed to take his phone with him. He did not know whether it was because – taking the time to reflect – he realised how much he missed his family and wished he saw more of them. No, you see Arthur knew, because being asleep with a waking body, he saw people differently to how you or I might look at them. To him, everyone was a symbol. They were simplified, and dream-like. There was something missing from this man, and Arthur knew what it was:

This man could sleep but he did not dream. Any dreams he had were broken ones, not fit for purpose, and not to be enjoyed. They did not serve the purpose that dreams should.

So Arthur decided to help. That night he took a walk to the man's subconscious. It took a long time: he had quite far to go to get there. You don't just arrive in another person's head, after all.

People's dreams take them to wherever they want to go. Arthur crossed through a few places he was familiar with, having worked there before.

He passed through the terrifying Realm of the Perpetual Tidal Wave, a vast beach front that varied depending on who was dreaming it, and whose defining trait was the colossal, impending black tidal wave that teetered on the edge of crashing down, bringing utter oblivion with it.

Rarely did the black wall crash – only a certain type of dreamer imagined that – and when it did, this would often bring consciousness with it. Arthur knew this, and used it as a shortcut, walking under the dark arch, its impending crashing shielding him from the sun.

Quite quickly day became night, as Arthur reached the end of the wave. The sea was peaceful here, the waters a frothing, inky blue under the starry night sky. Bubbles rose from the depths of the sea and parted from the waters, into the air, and Arthur rode them; the bubbles bulging as if overripe under his weight, yet failing to burst as he hopped from one to the other.

Crossing the sea, Arthur reached Grandmashouseland, an amalgamation of grandparent's houses that was somehow still one house, full of winding or impossibly long corridors; rooms one wasn't allowed to go in; enormous armchairs and things panelled with wood.

Leaving this land via the secret area under the tree in the back garden – there was always one – Arthur then hitched a lift on an aqua zeppelin, which was a bit like a blimp with an enormous fish in the place of the balloon, and eventually the Businessman's subconscious appeared on the curved horizon.

It was right where it should have been, outside the edges of interest, and beyond the borders of tediousness.

This explained a lot, he thought. The Businessman's mind resembled an office, but the dullest one imaginable, all grey and devoid of texture, yet somehow not smooth. The closest thing it seemed like – although Arthur wouldn't have known this – was an old and incomplete computer programme, poorly rendered. The sky was black; not because it was night, but because it hadn't been designed. It was unfinished.

The office stretched in every direction, a labyrinth of mediocrity and the unexceptional, utterly silent.

Arthur had seen things like this before, where imagination was replaced by crushing routine and schedules, but not to this extent.

He knew something had to be done, so he built a dream for the Businessman that was worth having.

He sculpted it from time and memory, from a palette of feelings, heavy in hues of wonder. It contained the impossible, the improbable, the unlikely, and the achingly familiar to create something astonishing and intimate. Arthur had never made a dream before; he was not a weaver but someone who maintained, a gardener, who appreciated the shapes made. But all in all, he thought he did okay.

But the world wouldn't hold. Something was wrong; dreams have a sort of glue to them, and in the Businessman's mind it was missing. Nothing would hold together.

Arthur realised there was a reason the dream wouldn't hold: if you don't make it yourself, you can't believe in it. It meant that the

Businessman had to help him in order for Arthur to help the Businessman. The irony was not lost on him.

So Arthur sought his help. The next day he approached him in the gardens, but being asleep, he struggled to make himself understood.

"You need more glue!" he told the Businessman. "The fabric won't hold!"

The Businessman – very politely, it must be said – told Arthur he understood when really he didn't, and decided for once to cut his lunch break short. He had emails to send and invoices to file.

Even asleep, Arthur knew he had failed.

He knew the only way this could work was for Arthur to wait until the Businessman was asleep, and sneak back into his mind. As the Businessman had no real dreams of his own, Arthur would have to take him into other people's to show him how to do it.

When he returned to the Businessman's mind, Arthur found him thinking he was at work, struggling to get anything done. Unawares that he was asleep, he was repeating the same problems over and over and not getting very far. When Arthur dream-napped him, he did not seem to mind one bit.

Arthur took him on a tour of other people's dreams, the very best he could find. The Businessman saw some truly amazing and touching sights, but he did not understand what Arthur was trying to show him. He told him as much.

"If they can do it, so can you," Arthur explained, relieved he was able to be understood here.

"No, I can't," the Businessman moaned, "I don't know how."

"Yes, you do," Arthur told him. "Everyone does. You've only forgotten."

Arthur spent some time trying to get the Businessman to dream. He tried to get him to grow simple things like sand castles and money trees, but the Businessman couldn't do it. Arthur knew drastic action was needed.

He took the Businessman up somewhere very, very high, and pushed him off, following shortly afterwards. He screamed the whole way down, while Arthur called over the rushing winds to do something about it. They would fall forever, if necessary. This dream would take as long as needed, time would be folded in order to be contained in one night.

When the Businessman made himself a giant umbrella, and sat panting and exhilarated in the crook of the handle, Arthur knew he had it. Together, they slowly drifted earthwards, where the ground now appeared below, ready to eventually meet them.

So Arthur brought the Businessman back to his own dream, and his companion realised what he was failing to imagine. Spread sheets, invoices and emails; schedules, deadlines and reports; these were things for the waking world. Let dreams be dreams.

Together, they started simple, building shapes, then buildings, becoming more impossible as they grew confident, until together they made a dream worth having.

It would be a place that could be calm, with lush meadows and glittering rivers, dotted with unusual follies or pagodas both grand and simple and unable to be conceived by the waking mind. There would be space for his children to play, for him to charm his wife. With waterfalls that went every direction except down, mountains made of colour, and beaches with silver sands and a glittering shore. It would be his, and it was whatever he needed.

The Businessman slept very well from then on.

Sometime later (Arthur did not know how long, he could not read clocks in the waking world, let alone calendars) he saw the Businessman again in the gardens. He looked happier, and Arthur could tell he was sleeping and dreaming.

The Businessman watched Arthur with a glimmer of recognition. He rationalised that after being approached by him, this strange fellow must have stuck in his mind and appeared in his dream. Nothing strange about that, right? Somehow it felt like more.

The Businessman never thanked Arthur; he couldn't prove anything, and besides, he didn't have to. Arthur was just doing his job. It might be more than he normally did, but sometimes you have to go above and beyond when it matters. Life went on, and the Businessman, like many others, continued to spend his lunchtimes in the gardens, although no longer for his health. Just because he could.

But years later, when the gardens were purchased by a big company who wanted to build over them, another company intervened, one whose branding bore an unmistakeable resemblance to the one the Businessman worked for. The gardens were preserved and left untouched, with only a few changes made…

… and Arthur was pleased to see a little more dream in their design.

Learn (Or: The Nice Apocalypse)

How was it done, by wish or by prayer?
The Earth itself had decided to care.
The world had slept, and by dawn's first light
Terrific changes had come through the night.

Ten thousand years passed, and come what may
None of us had aged, not even a day.
What had changed was the world at hand,
It had fought back; it had made a stand.

Giant trees loomed in unexpected places,
No more Wembley Stadium, no more Ascot races.
The car parks were meadows, construction yards orchards,
Who would we fight, who would be tortured?

Oil rigs suspended in newly set ice,
The icebergs had expanded, doubling, twice.
Scarce beasts returned to lands they had lost,
And man saw the beauty progression had cost.

But what caused this change, we wanted to know,
What had made the seas clean, what had made the trees grow?
The only clue this, a word seen from space,
Left as a message for the human race.

Small islands arranged as a single word,

Spelling out "learn," now seen and heard.

Now the time's come to take a stance,

What should we do with our second chance?

What the Mystic Showed You:

Neptune in Eight Minutes

This is more like a vision, not quite a dream. Maybe this is the glimpse of infinity granted in the heartbeat before death, who can say? Memory before this moment is non-existent. Even identity is lost. Maybe this is my story, and I'm telling it. Maybe this is yours, and I'm describing what you see.

Just know this is happening, more or less.

It begins.


0:00

Passing through space faster than light, than thought itself, through distances vast and immeasurable. No man has travelled this far before. But then, where I, or you, or we are heading is no place for man.


0:15

Through the vastness of space, your destination approaches: we're slowing down. The planet is an exquisite blue marble, not so different from Earth. Yet as it grows, the comfort of familiarity ebbs away, and all that remains is mystery.

The blue orb fills your vision, and it is a colour that defies description. Dusty.

Ghostly. But pure, and limitless. You wonder at this curious ball, so lonely, lying at the end of all that is known: a sentinel on the cusp of infinity.

The blue: does it penetrate, the whole way through? Is it the inert sphere of gas it is believed to be, a decision made with telescopes and satellites? They have not been here. They have not seen it like you do now. There's something else in there.

There is more. There has to be.

Something waits.


0:45

The blue submerges you. It blinds us. Press on. Trust you are moving in the right direction.

Press on.

After an eternity of the blue, finally a variance occurs. Even the smallest change is noticeable: pure colour, whatever that is, is almost like pure darkness. Except the change that comes *is* dark, and has depth, texture. Surface. Something behind the blue, lying still, waits to be revealed.

It has waited long enough.

The mist parts to reveal the surroundings, but lingers, unwilling to expose itself entirely. Even as spirit this place is unwelcoming. Maybe it knows. We cannot let our guard down.


1:12

There's a tingling in us that I suspect is as much fear as it is curiosity, but you tell me.

In every direction is life, or what once resembled it, although only a dozen feet in any direction is visible. Rancid vegetation lies everywhere: ancient, dying trees that have succumbed to time, smothered in mist and what resembles vines, ivy and rot. They bend in the direction of defeat.

Everything screams of past lost; of a time long gone and left to decompose. But there *was* life here once. There was greatness. You can taste it.

But is anything left? Life remains, that much is clear, but what about intelligence? Is it sleeping, ready to be awakened? If it awakens, will it be dangerous?

Despite the ravages of time, a path remains. Small, neglected, overgrown, but proof. Something lived here. Now, we have to learn what.

Follow it.

The path, like everything else here, leads into the relentless blue mist. Without failing, it keeps going in a straight line, running through the ground of this wasted land.

The track widens. What was at first a well-trodden line broadens out, becomes developed. Paved. *Someone* made this path. Where are they now? What could have made them leave?

Follow.

1:55

The path seems to come to an end. It widens into a clearing, leaving me unsure where to go. The rancid vegetation seems unable to reach this clearing, but there's no explanation –

Oh

My

God

After an eternity of blue grey mist seeping into every corner, it clears, and the uncertainty is replaced with horror.

I've reached something. All roads lead here. In front of me is what must be a temple. It's grander in scale, yet more desolate than anything history has ever known.

It's immense.

There's something about the temple. Something terrifying. It's ingrained in the building, in the very stone.

Then I realise: this is only the tip of the iceberg. The temple expands all around, under my feet – either by design, or through millennia stood alone, the ground shifting around it, matter decaying around and on top of it.

It has survived all this. It is permanent.

Something incredibly intelligent made this place, something that knows nothing of morality.

We shouldn't have come here.

I want to run, but something (is it you?) holds me in place.

*Wait*! For what?

Let it pass. You'll see.

If we run now, we'll never know.

2:54

Know what?

We're not in any obvious danger. Take a moment. Have you ever seen anything like this before? We are privileged to see it. Who was the last living being to do so?

The feeling rises: awe. This is something bigger and older than mankind itself could ever dream of being, will ever be.

Something that surely must be dead, because nothing that remains of a civilisation so majestic would allow itself to be forgotten so easily.

We await instructions. A sign.

Nothing moves.


3:13

Nothing has to. Even in death, this culture has moved beyond language. It is *feeling*. Without moving, the world seems to shift, propels you forward. You are led to the foot of the temple. It is the only way forward.

A staircase, leading underground, and you realise what is leading you this way: light.

The first light since entering the blue mist that binds this world in mystery, the first sign that life may yet remain on this aloof place of rot and fallen dignity.

The light is green, and both natural and unnatural at once. Is it warm and right, or a siren, calling you to shipwreck?

It doesn't matter.

Follow, even if it means death.

3:40

We descend for what feels like miles. The steps are broad and worn, like an old cathedral's. Many have passed this way before. Where are they now?

The staircase narrows as you go, and even the ceiling lowers, forming a tunnel. This only makes the light brighter.

The decayed world behind you is forgotten.

Follow.

4:00

The cool green light is your only purpose now. You can feel it. The heart.

And something in the light calls to you; something familiar, and long forgotten, the memory only awakening now: a profound sense of importance, of something vital.

Something that knows nothing of good and evil, that just *is*. You don't care. You just remember.

How could I forget? How could any of us?

Further down now, the sleepy horror of above has truly gone, has been purged and left behind. Everything is clearer here. Our senses more alert. The stone of the steps becomes sharp; time has been unable to wear them away down here.

4:24

We are changing. Every layer of awareness peels off, burns away. Burn is right in only some ways. It must be the green light that is changing us, but there's no heat you feel. It's the light.

It echoes and moves. Can light echo? Is that even possible? It feels like the only way to describe it: an echo and a pulse.

The steps end, finally, as does the tunnel, opening out into a chamber.

A first it seems limitless, stretching on and out for miles in every direction, including above. How can that even be possible? My mind tells me I'm deep underground, but every sense I have tells me otherwise. The air is cool and pure, but I'm not cold. I'm not anything but curious.

Then a swelling grows in my core. The light. I'm close now, it's just ahead, and as I get closer it dawns on me that there's no reason to be afraid.

There's no reason to be afraid of anything.

One final obstruction remains, a small one. Leading into the huge room (if that's what this is) is a small flight of steps, obscuring my goal, and as I reach the top, the sight is revealed to me.

At the same time, without realising, I release every anxiety locked in me. Every need, worry or concern, no matter how deeply buried. Even those I never knew I had, those that are so integral to me, are gone.


4:55
Peace.

There's no mistake: the light is beauty. It's the warm glow at the centre. It resides in the heart of everything, but is forgotten in a world populated by miracles.

Only here, at the end of everything and against the stark backdrop of nothing, can it be seen in the literal sense, without concealment or metaphor.

This isn't profane.


5:15

It's sacred. Nothing is dead, because there is no death. Even the world above has a purpose, to nurture the purity down here.

I feel calm.

And I see the source of the light. It's not blinding but as tranquil as the light it emanates, yet powerful and terrible nonetheless. Held back by a universal judgement and an absolute will.

At the end of the chamber, the far wall is comprised entirely of a something massive, glowing and green; the substance it must be comprised of defies the mind. Is it a colossal wall of water, suspended in the air? Or is it fire, burning without heat and somehow leaving its surroundings unscathed?

Somehow, it's both and neither.

This is The Source.


5:30

With nothing further between you and The Source, you come to understand. Sacred is profane, and profane is sacred.

The pulsing and echo of the light changes, or to be precise, opens up, and its true sound is heard.

Voices.

The pulses become a choir, thousands strong, the voices a contradiction; human and otherworldly; beautiful and strong, wailing and terrible.

You are seeing the centre. Something unfathomable. You could stay forever, with all of its secrets to learn.

Yet as we are prepared to let go and lose all sense of self, to surrender to oblivion, another change, one that holds you back.

We are noticed.


6:13

We have looked too long, and somehow The Source has seen you staring.

This is not an intelligence that can be understood, it is not tame, and it has a judgement and an intellect that something as small as we are can never truly begin to comprehend. Even with all sense of self stripped away, we are still a blemish on its purity. We are not ready.

We have seen, but something we shouldn't. When its attention turns to you, only for a heartbeat, do you understand how terrible its majesty truly is.

You understand:


6:34

You cannot stay. You will not remember, not in your conscious mind at any rate, no matter how much you wish you could. But your soul may. In the deepest of dreams, wrapped in images and metaphor in order to understand it, you may feel in the depths of your unconscious that you have struck something deep and pure, but are unable to articulate it, so that only a small sadness remains to undermine a feeling of contentment that should be enough.

And maybe one day, when the stars breathe their last and all light is gone, will the universe see this last bastion of purity, keeping hope alive.

Without moving, we are leaving.


7:00

It fades now. You struggle to remember, but only flashes remain. Carried up and out, through the rock and earth, the temple disappears beneath our feet before being consumed by the mist – green now, not blue – the planet drops away as we move through the atmosphere and away from the planet, through the expanses of the universe so fast it feels as if you are hardly moving at all. With no mass, we feel no resistance.


7:40

Until finally, you, I, we

Wake up.

# The Duke's Departure

When the Duke passed, no one knew if it was true or not.

He had played the jester, spun many tales for so long, this was exactly his sort of thing.

Some people searched, and others asked.

I just waited. There would be sources you could trust.

And the news came in, from those who wouldn't lie about such things.

So there it was, cannot argue with that. Gone is gone.

But I could not help but hope that it was a most intricate web of lies, weaved over a lifetime.

To distract us from the greatest trick of all.

Helen and Jim were a perfectly normal couple. They were perfectly normal in that they were both mad, neurotic, insecure and uncertain individuals, but it didn't matter because they had each other, and together they made a complete whole that passed for normal.

Everything was as it should be.

And so it was that their wedding day approached. As with all couple's wedding days, it seemed an eternity in coming, yet somehow arrived in no time at all. They were very organised (well, one of them was, but I won't say which) but perhaps inevitably some details were left to the last minute.

"We need a GPS," Helen told Jim over the phone in the final week before the wedding. She worked away from home a lot, and with the wedding drawing ever nearer, the responsibility to pick up items and run errands fell to Jim.

They needed a GPS because the wedding was in Wales, and like most places in Wales, there seemed to be no way for phone data to work which rules out map apps, and it was nearly impossible to find your location unless you had been there before, or had someone telling you where to go. A GPS counted as the latter.

I should probably clarify something here; a note on memory and truth which neither party can quite agree on. Helen believed she told this to Jim well in advance, and he forgot to do it. This was typical of Jim, who also forgets to call his friends enough. In contrast, Jim had no memory of Helen mentioning this, and believes his fiancé *thinks* she mentioned this, but actually didn't. This too is typical of Helen. The debate continues to this day.

Either way, it was the day before they were due to drive to Wales, and no GPS had been purchased. Jim had frantically taken to the streets to acquire one; their last GPS having never quite worked correctly since Jim had downloaded a new voice for it. "The Shatnav," he proudly called it, ever since it took on the voice of a certain former Star Trek captain.

If Jim believed in such things, he would have said that fate was conspiring against him – every shop in town that should stock them either having run out, or was closed.

In fact, Jim had all but given up, and decided to console himself by checking out the books D. Jones's, a local charity shop. He hadn't visited this charity shop before – in fact he hadn't even noticed it, which was strange as both he and Helen were avid charity shop goers – but given the lack of books, he realised he wasn't missing out. The whole shop seemed to stock nothing but nautical themed items and smelled faintly of brine.

"Can I help you with something?" came a gruff voice from behind the counter. It belonged to a ruddy faced, straggly bearded old man who looked remarkably out of place in a Surrey charity shop. Perhaps the only place he would look at home would be a remote fishing village somewhere.

"I'm fine, thanks," Jim said as he walked out, but he paused on the threshold. Maybe it was desperation – who can say – but what the hell, "I don't suppose you have any satnavs?" he asked, getting only a blank look in response. "GPS?" he clarified.

The man looked thoughtful for a moment and considered the question. Jim doubted he even knew what a GPS was, and was going to tell him not to bother, when the man's voice boomed like Richard Burton doing Hamlet, "The map things! I know! Technology today, eh?" he paused and looked hard at Jim. "What's wrong with a map, eh sonny? They've been doing right by people for centuries."

Jim couldn't argue with that. "It's to get to our wedding," he explained, "My fiancé –"

"Right! Got it!" the old man interrupted, holding his hands up in a gesture of submission. "Weddings and wives to be. What man can stand in the way of that dread combination? You might as well ask the tide not to come in."

Jim nodded politely, racking his brains for a way out of the conversation, when the shopkeeper informed him they may have one out the back.

He went to look immediately, muttering to himself as he did so. Jim suspected he was humming a sea shanty. He was gone a long time, and Jim was just about ready to sneak off, politeness be damned, when that voice boomed, "Thar she is!"

The old man emerged clutching what *could* be a GPS in his stubby fingers; a coil of cable wrapped limply around it. "It might not be the most presentable, but I tested it myself. Works a treat. It'll find north for ya."

"How much do you want for it?" Jim asked, beyond unsure by this point.

"Consider it a wedding present," the shopkeeper beamed, placing the device in Jim's hand. It felt strange: it had the dry texture of dead starfish.

Jim thanked the rather strange old man, donated a fiver because it seemed like the thing to do, and went on his way. He couldn't help but feel that there was something fishy about the shop owner, but he couldn't work out what.

*

The next day, car packed, the soon-to-be-married couple were ready to go. They were understandably nervous – this time tomorrow they would be getting married, after all. So Helen sadly did not see the funny side when Jim struggled to set up the GPS.

"What's *that*?" she frowned.

"It's the satnav," Jim offered as casually as he could.

"If you say so," she said, one eyebrow arched suspiciously.

"It was the only one they had!"

"Who's the 'they' in that sentence?" she asked, suspecting Jim's search might not have been as thorough as she had expected.

"It'll get us there," Jim assured her, deciding to leave the charity shop out of it. Doubts were starting to gnaw at him too. The GPS was incredibly resistant to instruction and toggling through the various menus, he couldn't find the screen to input their destination. One would've thought it would be the most obvious one, given that this was its sole purpose, but apparently not.

"Well, we know how to get to Wales at least," Helen shrugged, trying not to show her frustrations.

"You have selected your destination: Whales," the satnav declared in a booming voice that made them both jump. They laughed – mostly from nerves – but also because the satnav's voice shared the same barnacle encrusted brogue of the man from the charity shop. There were better voices one could assign to a GPS.

They set off. Their journey was uneventful for the most part to begin with; as they shot down the M4 with only one stop for services and a disappointing breakfast. The roads were surprisingly quiet and the weather was ideal for a wedding, warm but with the foreshadowed coolness of autumn that September always hinted at.

As they crossed the Severn Bridge, Helen suggested having another go with the GPS. The A449 has closures and the road was rather crucial to them reaching their destination, and without the benefit of the satnav they would be flying blind.

"Bloody thing," Jim mumbled, rather regretting the purchase by this point.

"Is it broken?" Helen asked, blood pressure rising.

"It's *crap*," Jim clarified, but then remembering who he was talking to – and what her stress levels were likely to be on the day before her wedding – added, "But I'll fix it, don't worry. It's recognised every road so far, I'm just struggling to add our destination."

"Destination!" boomed the satnav with the same thunderous sea dog voice as before. "Where do yer want to go?"

"Oh, it's voice activated!" Jim realised. "That's cool."

"Why's it sound like a pirate?" Helen asked.

"I dunno," Jim said, omitting the man from the charity shop. "Maybe it's a download?" He told the satnav the name of their location.

The GPS did nothing. Jim frowned, and reached for the brochure for the wedding venue, looking for the map.

He repeated the name of the location, careful of getting the pronunciation right. No answer. "Useless."

"Try some of the surrounding roads," Helen suggested, thinking it might be best to leave him to it.

Jim gave it a go, trying half a dozen roads in the vague area of the venue. No joy.

"You can hardly blame it," Helen said, the voice of reason to Jim's increasing frustration.

"Why's that?" Jim asked, exasperated.

"Well, you do mumble," she teased.

"I don't mumble," he protested. "Everyone else is just deaf."

*

The further they travelled, the more signs they saw announcing that the road they wanted was closed. The sense of importance this placed on Jim felt almost palpable as he realised without the A40 they were running out of road.

"Speech House Road," he tried.

"Road not known."

"Church Road."

"Road not known."

"Poolway Road," Jim said, calling out the name of any road he could find that was nearby.

"Poolway Road."

"Um, did it just recognise that one?" he asked.

"Poolway Road *via* Whales?" the GPS asked.

"Yes!" Jim almost yelled into the device, "We're going to Wales! We're *in* Wales!"

"So, Poolway Road via Whales. Confirm course, Captain."

"Confirmed," Jim sighed, exasperated, rubbing his eyes with his palm.

A bright blue line appeared on the GPS immediately: their route was locked in.

"Well, it's not perfect, but it's closer than we are now."

"Head west in a mile," the GPS told them.

"West?" Helen frowned. "Left or right?"

Jim played with the device for a few moments, until the satnav declared, "Turn to port in 0.9 miles."

"Left or right!" Jim ordered.

"Yar," the GPS agreed, actually sounding disappointed. "Left turn in 0.9 miles."

Despite their initial grumblings, the GPS actually proved both remarkably useful and accurate, handling the obscure country roads with ease. It did, however, have a tendency to mispronounce the roads that it took them down.

'Coalway' for instance, was 'Shoal Way.' 'Speech House Road' was 'Beach House Road.' It didn't struggle with 'Bream' or 'Beech Grove' though.

"It's taking us an odd way," Jim observed, looking at their map. They were headed south, towards the coast, and as far as he could tell, away from the venue. "Must be 'cos of the diversion," he added, not wanting to worry Helen more than he already had.

If nothing else, their route had taken them via some stunning scenery; the rolling hills and carpeted green valleys parted with shimmering blue seams of river were constant reminders of why they had chosen Wales to get married in in the first place. Their route took them up what resembled a mountainous pass, winding and twisting as it ascended, and neither of them knew where it led.

"Where's satnav say to go after this?" Helen asked.

"Um…" Jim said, "I'm not sure."

"Not sure?"

"The route goes kinda funny," he said, scrutinising the GPS display intensely. As far as he could see, the route *ended* shortly ahead, but they were miles from the venue, yet this was where the GPS told them to go.

"Maybe it'll make sense after this tunnel," Helen hoped.

"What tunnel?" Jim asked, still focusing on making sense out of the satnav. He glanced up, and just as Helen had said, the road disappeared into a black hole in the hillside. They both noticed how strange the tunnel's roof was before the darkness consumed them.

Helen turned the headlights on, but it seemed to make little difference. They slowed right down.

"Jim… " she murmured, worry edging into her voice.

He shared her concerns.

The GPS compounded it.

"Take the whale," it said, as the way shut behind them.

*

"It said whale, didn't it?" Helen observed, with odd detachment.

"Yeah," Jim agreed, "That can't be right. I mean, what sort of whale just waits in a tunnel with its mouth open, anyway?"

"Seriously? That's your biggest problem with this?"

It shouldn't have been. The car was beginning to wobble: the ground under them was moving. Unbeknownst to them, the whale had slid back out of the tunnel and entered the sea, submerging deep underwater. Even within the whale they could hear water splashing around them.

They looked around in vain, although they knew they wouldn't find a way out.

"Maybe we could ram our way out," Jim thought aloud. "Turn the engine on."

The car had stalled when they entered the tunnel, and Helen turned it back on, the Toyota coming to life and its headlights illuminating the inside of the whale's mouth.

From around them came a deep, heavy coughing sound, and a very loud, deep voice boomed, "STOP THAT!"

They looked at each other in alarm. "Who said that?" Jim asked, winding down the window.

"I'd do as he says," said another voice, tinnier but more immediate and stranger.

"Do as who says?" Helen replied.

"The whale, stupid," the second voice answered.

"Who is that?" Helen called out, "Who's there?"

"We'll discuss that later," the voice said. "You've got bigger problems."

"I SAID: STOP THAT!" the whale boomed, and it shook from side to side, throwing the couple about in their car.

"Or," Jim shouted back at the whale, "We could keep the engine running and smoke you out. It would be tricky for you to hold your breath while your lungs fill with petrol fumes."

"THIS CONVERSATION BORES ME," the whale answered immediately. "WHEN I'M BORED, I YAWN. WOULD YOU LIKE TO SEE HOW MUCH WATER ENTERS MY MOUTH WHEN I YAWN?"

They looked at one another, then turned the engine off. They kept the headlights on though; that was the only thing keeping them from utter blackness.

"THAT'S BETTER," the whale voice said all around them.

"A smart arse whale," Jim remarked. "Great."

He opened the car door and stepped out. Reluctantly, Helen did the same. The ground under their feet was soft and squelchy.

"How come it speaks English?" Helen wondered aloud.

"It always speaks English," the smaller, second voice said.

"Really?"

"You only understand it because it's clearer. It's easier to understand when you're in its mouth rather than through water," the voice explained. "Outside, it sounds like squealing gibberish."

"And what are you then?" Jim asked, dreading the answer, "A talking crab?"

"We are krill."

"Of course you are."

"What sort of fish are you?" the krill asked, its voice made up of hundreds of tiny voices, all speaking in unison. The krill were dotted around the whale's mouth in small pools. Helen, Jim, and their car were all rested on the whale's tongue, and were for the most part kept out of the water. "I wonder how it speaks with us on its tongue," mused Jim.

"If you're going to keep asking stupid questions you're going to give yourself a headache," the krill informed them. "Not that it matters – you've been eaten – it's the stomach for you."

"Eaten?" Helen gasped, "No! You can't! We're getting married tomorrow!"

"Not up to us, love," the krill said, and a thousand tiny creatures shrugged as one.

"WHAT IS MARRIED?" the whale asked.

"It's when two people decide to spend the rest of their lives together," Helen told the whale.

"HAVE YOU NOT DECIDED THIS ALREADY?" the whale enquired.

"Well, we live together," Helen said, "But it's not quite the same –"

"EXPLAIN."

"I'm trying but you keep interrupting!" she snapped, before remembering who she was talking to and forcing herself to be calm. "It's a ceremony," she explained, "In front of the people we love, to show them how much we care for each other, and to celebrate it."

"Sounds expensive," chittered the krill, which was strange as they had no concept of money.

"You don't know the half of it," Jim agreed, but quickly shut up when Helen shot him a withering look.

"CEREMONIES DON'T MATTER," the whale told them. "I'M STILL GOING TO EAT YOU."

"But – you can't!" Helen protested, "Not now! It took me so long to get a cake I wanted, and the bridesmaid dresses – they're all so different, it was nearly impossible to get one design that suited them all!" She felt herself getting tearful now. Helen had figured that tears would be shed around their wedding day, but she didn't think it would be for *this* reason.

"SOME THINGS ARE BEYOND YOUR CONTROL," the whale said. "NOW PREPARE TO BE DIGESTED."

"Come off it!" Jim shouted, his voice incredibly clear, echoing through the whale's cavernous mouth. "We're getting married tomorrow and that's that! Do you know how long it took me to find a woman like her? They don't grow on trees you know!"

"STILL EATING YOU," the whale declared.

"Fine," Jim answered, "But if you eat us, we'll climb back out again and have this argument over and over."

"WHAT ARGUMENT?"

"Why we deserve to get married," Helen chipped in, also getting stuck into the debate.

"They sound pretty determined," the krill observed, "We never make this much fuss when we're eaten."

"That's because there's thousands of you," Helen argued. "There's only two of us."

"SOON THERE WILL BE NONE OF YOU."

"You're a berk," Jim told the whale.

"Haven't you ever known anyone like that?" Helen asked it. "Isn't there anyone you wanted to spend your life with?"

"I…"

"There was, wasn't there?"

"THIS ONLY MAKES ME WANT TO EAT YOU FASTER."

"What did you do to lose it?" Jim asked, understanding what Helen was trying. They had attempted reason, then threats, now they decided to try understanding.

"I… I DON'T REMEMBER," the whale lied. Then, "THERE MIGHT HAVE BEEN A FEW REASONS."

"Tell us."

"YOU'RE TRYING TO TRICK ME."

"If you're going to eat us anyway, we might as well know why."

"SHE WANTED EVERYTHING TO BE DONE A CERTAIN WAY, AND I DIDN'T SHOW THAT I CARED ENOUGH," the whale paused, "OR MAYBE IT WAS THE OTHER WAY ROUND."

The human morsels shared a look. "Sounds understandable."

"OH," the whale said, "AND HOW HAVE YOU TWO MANAGED THIS?"

"We make it work," Helen said. "That's what you do when you love each other. That's why we're getting married."

"AND DOES IT WORK?"

"Mostly."

"HOW?"

"Patience. Understanding. You have to work at it."

"HMM," the whale made a deep, thoughtful sound, "I DON'T THINK I WANT TO EAT YOU NOW."

"That would be nice."

"YOU'VE MADE ME LOSE MY APPETITE. SICKENING."

"We're not that tasty. And car can't possibly be good for you."

They were all silent for a while, the only sounds the sloshing of water in the whale's mouth, and the infrequent chittering of the krill.

"So… what now?" Jim asked.

"YOU TWO REALLY LOVE ONE ANOTHER?"

"Yes," they said.

"PROVE IT."

"How?"

"GET MARRIED. HERE. NOW."

"We – we don't have a registrar, witnesses –"

"DON'T CARE. GETTING HUNGRY AGAIN."

"Better go through with it," the krill advised, "He's getting surly."

They decided the krill was probably right. If the choice was between getting married in the mouth of a whale, and being eaten, it wasn't the hardest choice they'd ever had to make.

Being a whale, the whale didn't know anything about wedding ceremonies, so they were spared having to get dressed up (although being in his mouth, he wouldn't have known anyway.) In fact, they were able to skip a lot of details, which was probably for the best as they were too on edge to really think creatively about how best to mock up a wedding in a whale's mouth in no time at all.

At least… at first. It was strange, but once the reality dawned on them as to what they were up to, their fear vanished. They were getting married in a whale. Who in the world can claim to have done that? They were already a unique couple. This just proved it all the more.

So, serenaded by the harmonies of a thousand krill – who somehow knew a surprisingly broad range of love songs – Helen walked down the aisle (tongue) to the registrar's table (car) where her fiancé was waiting for her.

They exchanged vows which – having no one to prompt them – were awkward but sincere, and won't be repeated here; mostly because they were deeply personal, but also because Jim would make a detrimental comment if he heard them repeated.

But they were said with meaning, and with love, and they would remember them for the rest of their lives, because, in the whale's mouth, they were the only two people in the world.

*

"Well… that's done," Jim said, after the krill instructed him to kiss the bride. How the krill knew this was anyone's guess.

"YES," the whale agreed. Its voice was thick with emotion. If they didn't know any better, they would say he was getting tearful.

"The big softy," the krill tittered.

"So, if it's all the same to you, we'd quite like to go," Helen suggested kindly. "People are going to be wondering where we are."

"HMM? OH… YES, I SUPPOSE."

"Maybe you could let us out somewhere?"

"OH, VERY WELL," it said, "WHERE DO YOU NEED TO GO?"

Helen gave him the location, adding, "But it's not exactly accessible from the sea."

"He could spit you out?" the krill prompted.

"Um, I don't think that's the safest of options," Jim said warily.

"NONSENSE. LEAST I CAN DO. ANY IDEA ROUGHLY WHERE IT IS?"

"I know!" chipped in the satnav, to both Helen and Jim's surprise.

"Oh, *now* you know?" Helen asked incredulously.

"I didn't understand at first," the satnav explained. "Your man mutters a bit. The acoustics in here make him easier to understand."

"Oh shut up," Jim said.

They piled into the car, and once they were ready, the satnav told the whale where to aim and how hard to spit. They felt the enormous animal shift and squirm as it adjusted itself. The car started to roll back as they realised the whale's tongue was gathering up behind them, its enormous body rising to the surface and tilting so its mouth was pointing upwards.

"THITH MIGHT BE A BIT BUMTHY," he said with a noticeable lisp. Apparently having a car resting on his tongue didn't impede his speech, but preparing to spit did. I don't know, I don't make this stuff up; if it doesn't make sense, ask a whale next time you're in its mouth.

"Okay," Helen said, then added, "Thanks for not eating us. Maybe you could go find your mate and make it work?"

"SHE'D PWOBABLY BE IMPWESSED WITH ME FOR THITH," the whale agreed. "HOLD ON."

It opened its mouth, and the newlyweds were nearly blinded and deafened as sunlight rushed in to meet them and water roared all around them, exploding under the whale's mighty path. As it opened its mouth, it spat them out in the same movement, sending the car high into the air in a trajectory towards their wedding venue.

The view was magnificent, but they didn't really appreciate it at the time. Instead, they screamed. It was hardly very dignified, but to be fair at the time, it must have seemed like certain death.

The car started its descent and began to plummet earthwards.

"Don't worry," the GPS assured them, its seafaring brogue rising over the screams. "I told you, I gave him the right directions."

The GPS wasn't lying. They were headed towards the downwards slope of a very steep hill, its angle matching their descent. "I'd turn your vessel on, if you would," the GPS advised. "If you can get up to at least fifty miles an hour it'd be best."

Helen did so, stamping her foot down and quickly getting the wheels spinning.

"Land, ho!" the satnav yelled, as the vehicle touched down, the tyres screaming as they hit the road with an almighty bump.

Helen struggled to retain control of the vehicle, but she held her nerve, fighting with the steering wheel until she reined the car in. Quite sensibly, they pulled over, both as white as sheets. Or the Welsh, who themselves are pretty pale.

"Well," Jim smiled, trying to stop his hands from shaking, "That was… different."

"Yeah," his wife agreed, "Should we… (she smiled) want to go get married?"

"Again?" he smiled, eyebrow arched.

"Sure."

And so they did. They drove (uneventfully, it must be said) to their wedding venue, which was every bit as beautiful as they had hoped it would be. And the next day, in front of all their friends and family, they committed to spending the rest of their lives with one another. Their day was perfect.

They never told anyone about what had happened on their drive down, because, quite simply, the events with the whale were quite preposterous, and no one in their right mind would believe it.

Whales don't talk. Krill doesn't either. And the satnav had discreetly slipped away shortly after they arrived safely, so they couldn't even prove that.

But that was okay. They were married now, the only ones who had to believe the things they said were each other. They had lived through something amazing, twice, in two days.

And that was their weddings in Wales.

Afterward

I really wasn't sure whether to write an introduction to this or not. I'm still unsure, which is why this makes its appearance at the end. The writers I love tend to include them, and I lap them up, desperate to learn a little bit more about their thoughts and their approach to writing. I don't have as much to say or share as they do, (and I strongly suspect people don't have as much of a burning desire to learn my inner thought processes) but I do think these sort of things make a collection more personal, and this has definitely been that to me, given that this is around fifteen years' worth of short stories in one place.

Moreover, I think a small degree of context can make you see stories in a completely different light, and in some instances, I wanted to share some credit.

So, without further ado:


**Sign of the Chimes**

I wanted a story to put the Mean Tales set into context and had this tale in mind for something else. It didn't take much to merge them. It might be my favourite one in the collection once I started fleshing it out, mostly because it took me by surprise, although I suspect I'll say that again later on.


**Sodor and Gomorrah**

This was my first entry to Create 50's *Twisted 50* competition and I'm delighted to say that it was published in the final fifty stories that mad up their collection. The railway crossing is in Crowthorne where I grew up and is real, albeit now decommissioned, replaced by a restored older bridge. It's the story that most people who've read my stuff talk to me about. Can't imagine why.

## The Vacant Field

Another *Twisted 50* finalist (vol 2, this time) that didn't make it to the published fifty but may make it into a later volume, based on what they were saying. We'll see. I like this one. It's like a horror story but without a villain. Or the villain is a field, which I think is probably rare. You don't get a lot of evil fields in literature. They tend to take a relatively passive role.

## The Four

Another published *Twisted 50* entry, (this got in while *The Vacant Field* didn't) and another kids' show reimagined. Some days I worry I'm starting to pigeonhole myself. I'm okay with that as long as the rights holders don't think I've encroached on their formats.

The one thing I would say about this is I enjoyed writing these little vignettes linked by these creatures as opposed to having a central protagonist. That was a lot of fun. My screenwriting lecturer would probably tell me that's not the done thing though. Ah well. As long as people are entertained.

**Control Eye**

When I started making notes for this, I pictured it like a *Black Mirror* tale, almost exclusively from Evelyn's point of view. I quickly realised that wasn't going to be how this would play out, at least not within the confines of the duration of a short story. I think the Donna/Abaddon stuff works quite nicely though. To me it felt more original that watching Evelyn inevitably sink into chaos and despair, but that's just like, my opinion, man.

**The Last Horror Movie**

Okay, so the cat bit did happen to me for real at my parent's house, and I still blame my brother, the shit.

This is my second Crowthorne story. The spooky bit at The Chase is real, too. This story is probably the most honest I've been about horror and hopefully articulates the way it gets under my skin.

**The Hanging Tree**

The story of the family allegedly hanging from the trees "happened" in Ambarrow woods, not far from the railway crossing of *Sodor and Gomorrah*. The reference to Tom is one of a few indications of the shared world these stories exist in.

We've been up that hill scores of times, both as kids as well as adults when on hikes. We've acted more immature on the latter.

That being said, I fell off that rope swing when I was fifteen or sixteen. Lost all pigment in one of my arms for a few years where I burned it, and a small bald patch under my chin. Worth it.

**White Clay Men**

This was a story that my friend Alan O'Connell told me about, telling me it came to him in a dream. He's fine. Really.

My first draft of this ended with the narrator saved, revealed to be a near-death experience of a Titanic survivor. Feedback from the people around me preferred it dark, which suits this fine as it loosely fits the *Mean Tales* framing better without the Titanic setting. I think I know some strange people.


**The Last Chime**

This started life as a mash up/wrap up story for the creepy reinterpretations of kids shows, but like all good things, took on a life of its own.

My friend Rob Golding liked *Sodor and Gomorrah* and the train part of this story is a retelling of a dream he told me he had after reading it, which I liked and was eager to include in some form. It slightly worries me that *Sodor* made its way into his subconscious mind though. I'm not sure I'm comfortable having this level of influence.

The other kids shows referenced here are of course, *The Wombles*, *Button Moon*, and discreetly at the end, *Peppa Pig*. My initial plan for the *Peppa Pig* bit was going to be having them sing the Peppa Pig theme, but replacing the words with "two legs bad, four legs good," from *Animal Farm*. As clever as I thought it would be, there was *no way* that would slip past an intellectual property lawyer, so that was quickly nipped in the bud.

**A Date with Destiny**

My first ever story I came up with as a grown up (pipping *The Man Who Ends All Things*, from my *Space Suits* novel by about six months), this sat around unfinished for years. All I knew is I wanted someone to be harassed by fate. I never thought it would be over love.

This is also a bit longer than the other stories but I'm okay with that if you are.


**The Freedom Fighter**

Like *Sodor and Gomorrah* and *The Four*, this was published in a Create 50 collection, this time *Singularity 50*. I liked the transcript approach here, very freeing.

I should really thank Chris Jones and the whole Create 50 team for all their influence and inspiration. I'd written short stories before this, but there was something about their initiative which really forced me to up my game. The *Mean Tales* section of this book wouldn't exist without them inspiring it. Good people.


**Waiting for the Seven Forty-Five**

For about two years, my friend James and I got the same train to work. We didn't really know one another that well, (he was dating an old friend of mine, so it was a friend of a friend kind of scenario) and we've both acknowledged since that at first, we would've rather sat and read, rather than chatting. But (possibly out of British politeness) we didn't, and he went on to be one of my best friends, and groomsmen at each other's weddings.

The statue in question is of Nicholas Winton, who heroically smuggled dozens of children out of Czechoslovakia before the outbreak of the Second World War. Turns out he lived in Maidenhead (as do I) and has quite a presence there, as he should.


**As We Know It**

I'd like this to be a sort of one act play. It started life as a screenplay when I was doing my screenwriting MA, and it's followed me round since. I've always enjoyed the idea of multiple apocalypses happening at once.


**Cog**

Cog started life as a project for a machinema commission for a man who owned a second life company (don't ask). He gave me a theme, which was so obscure I can't really remember it now (it had to be about being a larger part of a whole, I think,) and I came up with something so convoluted that with one sentence, my friend Jim Powell was able to boil it down to what it should be: "What if he was a computer game character?"

Huh.

"Yeah, that'll do it, Jim…"


***Pong!***

My friend Matt Mills approached me about turning my short story *Norm's Attempt* into a radio play. Recording it was one of the most rewarding experiences I've ever experienced, and it got me thinking about what else I could write for radio.

*Pong* came about because I thought about that submarine radar sound effect, and how, as a kid, whenever I tried doing a Darth Vader impression, it sounded like that.


**A Biting Lie**

Most of this is actually a true story. I should have gone in the Green Book. But I'm not a vampire, honest.


**D.E.N.T.ist**

I originally wrote this as a screenplay about a boy and his father for my audition piece for Westminster University. Turns out, in the thirteen years since I wrote the screenplay, I've actually learned how to talk to kids and I guess it shows, because hardly a word of the parent's dialogue is the same since rewriting it. The dad (now mum) in the original draft spoke like Mr Banks from *Mary Poppins*, but worse.

Also, I've always been awful at coming up with acronyms, as this should attest.


**The Boastful Turtle**

This was written for something called the World Stories project, which looked at retelling folk tales for school children around the world. I'd written an original story (*Sow What*) and they liked it, so asked me to do one of the traditional ones. It was fun, and the project was great.


**Sow What**

This was the other World Stories project tale I submitted. I'm really fond of this story, and a couple of my friends gave me some nice pointers on it while I was preparing it. (Thanks James and Christian.) One day, maybe, I'll turn this into a full-length novel, just so I can illustrate it. I'd love to draw the What plant.


**The Dream Job**

I like the story about how this tale came together, simply because it's so odd. Alan O'Connell, mentioned above, contacted me out of the blue one day asking if I wanted to collaborate on a project; I do the writing, he does the visuals. His art is second to none, so of course I'm eager. His mate would help, and his mate's brother would even bind it. Even better.

The premise? A man who's asleep when awake, and awake when asleep. I could get behind that. Off to work.

Cut to some months later, and Alan and his mate are out owing to other commitments, but his mate's brother (Sam Harris) was still in. I go to meet him (having never met him before) and, it turns out, it's been explained to me backwards: he's already told this story, in fact, it's a very beautifully designed thirty-minute-long black and white film called *Arthur Sleep*. Oh.

So we both created the same story, but without even knowing it. I think Arthur would respect the symmetry.

On reflection, I think this story is a very loose companion piece to my *All Worlds Unseen* series. I like the idea Arthur is in the same world as Aurora and her friends, completely unnoticed by them.


**Learn (Or: The Nice Apocalypse)**

I don't know much about poetry. I know there's some amazing stuff out there, and I completely acknowledge this as my own ignorance rather than any fault that I can find in the medium.

*Learn* started off as an idea I had for a story, but truly I think poetry suits it best.

Also, I kinda think it would literally be the best thing to happen to the planet, but that's just me.


**What the Mystic Showed You: Neptune in Eight Minutes**

Okay, so bear with me here. I really like this, but when I describe it, there's always the risk you'll hear the sucking sound of me disappearing up my own backside.

I really wanted to get into classical music – still do, I haven't got far – and a couple of friends recommended *The Planets Suite*, by Holst. And yes, it's amazing. But I became obsessed by the last track, *Neptune*. I don't know why. I think I like how understated the piece is, and how it seems to tell a story. I got fixated on what that story was, and listening to it over and over, I came up with this.

Where things get interesting (or ridiculous, if you're sceptical about these things) is that in trying to work out what was happening when, I kept a note of the time line in my draft. These developed, and somewhere along the line I got this quite odd idea of trying to write this so the story read in real time. Which is stupid, obviously, as people read at different speeds. But I tried it anyway. (No one ever said writing was meant to be sensible.)

So there you have it. It's the world's first real time sci-fi set to classical music written in the second person.

You can't say I'm not ambitious.


**The Duke's Departure**

This was my entry in the Reader's Digest 100-word short story competition. David Bowie had died the month beforehand, so I wrote it for him.


**A Wedding in Wales**

This is the second of two whale stories in this volume. I don't tend to write whale stories, honest, and I probably don't have a third whale story in me.

This was written for two of my friends who got married in Wales, names slightly amended. To the best of my knowledge, no whales ate them on their route down. If they did, they kept quiet about it.

www.ingramcontent.com/pod-product-compliance
Lightning Source LLC
Chambersburg PA
CBHW051956150726
47999CB00004B/1407